THEORY

CARLOS

This is a publication of Machiavelli Productions LLC

ISBN-13: 9780578669885

The Library of Congress has cataloged the edition as follows:
Carlos
Theory: A Novel/Carlos First edition
1. Allegory-fiction 2. Alternative Universe-Fiction

Children will always be afraid of the dark, and men with minds sensitive to hereditary impulse will always tremble at the thought of the hidden and fathomless worlds of strange life which may pulsate in the gulfs beyond the stars, or press hideously upon our own globe in unholy dimensions which only the dead and the moonstruck can glimpse.

H.P. Lovecraft

The universe is change; our life is what our thoughts make it.

Marcus Aurelius

PROLOGUE

Darkness enveloped the well-worn dirt road, as if it weren't even there. It was there, that is for sure, but what was to happen in that darkness was such that unless you witnessed it yourself, you might question what had happened.

The wind picked up a bit, the type of breeze that one knows will accompany a storm. The wind howled, and there was a flash of localized lightning.

Inside there was a flash, too. The television flickered; its luminescence danced on the face of the old man passed out in his trusty beat-up recliner. A few drops of shitty scotch remained in the bottle that had slipped out of the man's hand. The bottle waited almost with a loyalty, waiting for its master to drain it.

The rest of the home was a hoarder's delight. Boxes of old, unwanted shit, much like the owner of the home, filled every nook and cranny. Yellowed newspapers stacked three-quarters to the ceiling appeared to be from at least fifty years past, but there were other things too. Like an indoor junkyard, crap was piled to the gills.

There were some things that seemed significant—a few photos of a younger version of the bag of bones that was passed out drunk in the moth-eaten chair, for one. The younger version was part of some sort of military group, standing ramrod straight, draped head to toe in midnight-black tactical gear, sometimes with another person wearing the same gear. It was unclear what organization or branch of the military these people in the photos were from, but it was definitely not a casual costume.

Outside, the lightning picked up and the winds swirled harder. The mailbox even moved a bit from the violence of the storm. The post that the box sits on was askew, and the force of the wind didn't help its stature. The metallic box that sat atop the post was nothing remarkable, but there was one thing that was odd: the box was black, but somehow there were darker letters on the box, almost hidden to an eye that might have passed it casually, yet they were undoubtedly there. The box read, "S. Black."

There was more lightning, but not light blasts emanating from the sky—it was local, and it was a preternatural red. It zipped almost unnoticeably at first, but it became more profound until something formed inside the intense red flashes. That something was hands. Large, powder-blue hands, covered in ruby-red tattoos, tore at the fabric of the universe. Out stepped the owner of the powder-blue hands, a massive behemoth of a man, nude and muscular. As he crossed from whatever world he came from, the tear in the universe repaired itself as if the creature had been there all along. He had not, but he was here now. The beast seemed to be getting his bearings. He looked at his arm, specifically at one of his tattoos. It was a clock, with Roman numerals, except instead of one to twelve, the clock only contained numbers one through eleven. The tattoo clock was in motion, changing its time from eleven to one. Once the tattoo clock stopped on the new time, the nude powder-blue man finally settled his eyes on the house where the flicker from the television could be seen. He made his way toward the door, and as he did, the largest of the symbols tattooed on the breadth of his back became visible. It was an Omega.

The creature lumbered up the walkway, almost as if he were a familiar guest coming back for another visit. His body was covered in archaic symbols, hieroglyphs, and numbers—one through eleven. Every muscle in his body was accentuated as he moved deftly to the door. The wind picked up, as if preternaturally supporting the advance of the Omega.

Inside, the old hoarder dozed unawares. He woke with a jolt when the door blew open with thunderous force. The man looked at the open door. There was nothing there. Except there was.

"Damn wind!" the old man yelled at the open door.

He got up gingerly, stiff from age, drunkenness, and immobility, but he was thrown back by the creature who exploded into the room with such speed and force that he could not comprehend it. The man tried to get up and make a run for it, but once again he was tossed like a rag doll back into the chair. Ribs were broken and the man in the chair struggled to breathe.

"What do you want?" the man asked.

When no answer came, the man with the broken ribs in the chair had a brief bout of hope—until he managed to pivot his aching neck and saw the Omega coming right at him. The wind picked up, and there was a thunderclap as the man howled, which masked his screams.

The Omega reached his target and as he did, the creature cocked his head, almost curious as to what his victim could possibly be experiencing. That didn't last long; the Omega helped the poor screaming man by opening his mouth wider, undoubtedly breaking his jaw as the creature slithered into the man's open mouth, and disappeared inside his body.

It was like the reverse of a snake that consumes a mouse. The man's body shook and flopped about as the nefarious creature did his horrific deed from the inside. Finally, the Omega reappeared the same way he had disappeared, but as he re-emerged from the man's mouth, the skin was all that was left. The Omega discarded the dermis like an unwanted coat to be donated to the Salvation Army, tossing its boneless sheath back on the chair, and then lumbered toward the mirror. The Omega tapped the tattoo watch on his hand and the number became animated and rotated from one to seven. He then climbed into the mirror as if it were liquid, disappearing into it. If not for the flayed skin of the owner of the home that rested like a shed snakeskin on the chair, one would have doubted that the Omega had been there at all.

PART ONE

CHAPTER 1

Elysium Theory lay in bed, passed out. Empty vodka bottles were strewn about the room as if he had thrown a massive party recently, but he hadn't. Theory was just a major drunk—a "functional alcoholic" was the correct term.

He hid his vice well. If you looked at his face, you would think that Theory was a fairly young man, in his thirties, but what could throw you off was the shock of almost albino white hair. Theory was forty-three years of age, at least biologically speaking. That said, some people are just older than their age. Elysium Theory's soul was weathered, beaten by a cosmic hurricane.

Theory's bedroom was festooned with bric-a-brac that showed off his professional success. There were posters from his show; one had Theory in silhouette, another had him passionately speaking into a microphone. Both posters had the slogan: "When we don't know, there is Theory." There were other posters advertising the show, which read: "New World Order is here!" "Government Secrets," "Trans-dimensional Events explained!" "Aliens live amongst us!"

Theory tossed and turned in his bed. He was in the throes of a nightmare, to be sure. It ended abruptly when Theory shot up suddenly, waking from whatever was haunting him. He was almost discombobulated as he wiped a bead of anxious sweat from his brow and his hollow cheeks. Theory got his bearings and threw off the bedding. He had been sleeping naked as he always did, and stretched briefly once he had risen. He lumbered bare-assed into the bathroom and brushed the foul taste of stale booze from his mouth.

The bathroom, like the rest of the flat, was elegant and modern. It wasn't as messy as the bedroom, but there were two vodka bottles sitting on the counter. One was empty, but the other was half full. Theory glanced at the bottle with some vodka left, but after brief contemplation decided against it; instead he started the rainforest shower. He looked at the bottle again. As if it were an old lover calling his name Theory stared, almost mesmerized, drawn to his coping mechanism.

Theory shook his head, snapping himself out of the hypnotic effect of the drink, and got into the shower. He let the water fall on him and imagined himself naked in the rain, which allowed him to relax for a brief moment. It was as if he were meditating, but then he wasn't alone. Female hands wrapped around Theory from behind. He smiled widely.

"I've missed you so much," he said.

"You have?" she asked.

"Desperately," he said, nodding.

Theory tried to turn around, but she didn't allow him.

"Please, let me see you," he begged.

"We only have a few precious seconds, love. To deviate from how it must be for now will only cost us time we cannot afford to give," she responded.

Theory closed his eyes. The unseen woman's hands wrapped around him tighter, almost in a quiet desperation. Finally, he couldn't take it anymore, and he moved ever so slightly—a twitch, if anything. Yet it was enough. Her hands fell away rapidly, and when Theory turned, there was nothing there except the tiles of the back of the wall in shower.

The man was distraught. He crumpled to the ground in a mixture of water and tears, as if someone had just stolen the last inch of his soul.

CHAPTER 2

Selena stared at the scene. She had been looking through the archives hoping for just this. Then again, no one could even have hoped for whatever this was.

Selena had raven hair, like the name all of her kind took. Black. She was twenty-eight years old, yet possessed the kind of beauty that would undoubtedly play over time. Selena Black glowed, almost as if she had stepped from the heavens, a goddess, incarnate. Yet that was the outside—on the inside she was one bad bitch, tough as they come, fearless in the face of any danger that her group faced.

The room in which Selena was working had a sterile look. Everything was metallic, from the desk where she sat to the massive monitor that she was studying the images on. Even the walls and the door seethed a silver sterility. It was for all intents and purposes a "clean" room. There was no need for it to be; this room was dedicated solely to AV research. Other rooms, more like labs, had different protocols where geeks in hazmat suits worked covertly. This clandestine location had no name. Some of the operatives who were allowed admittance called it the Center—a generic term, to be sure, but it covered what it was without giving anything away, as cloak and dagger places were wont to do.

Selena didn't turn at the hiss of the metallic pocket door opening. She didn't need to; no one who wasn't part of the organization would have access, and besides all that, Selena was focused on the imagery on the screen before her.

"What have you got there?" asked a deep voice from behind her.

"Looks familiar, no?" she said, finally turning.

The man focused on the screen. He was draped in black khaki pants and a button-down shirt, just as Selena was. Ott was a major in the organization, although the rank was not advertised in any way. The Black operation had a chain of command, but you wouldn't know it by looking at them. They were shrouded in mystery to anyone on the outside. Civilians had no idea who they were or what they did exactly, other than that if the Blacks were there, something bad and undoubtedly fucked up had happened.

Major Ott stood behind Selena. His look screamed "military." Short cropped hair to go along with the ramrod-straight posture gave him away. Ott was a Black legacy. The major was third generation; covert operations might as well have been in his DNA.

"It does look the same. Where did it materialize?" Ott asked.

Selena turned her attention back to the screen, the image was what appeared to be a skin, human.

"It isn't where, it's when," Selena told her superior.

"OK, when is it from?"

"1919."

"One hundred and ten years ago? This has been going on for that long? How could we have missed it?" Ott squinted at the screen.

"We just weren't looking, and back then no one would have known what to make of it anyway."

"Good point. Any ideas on the skin?" the major asked.

"Not from the research. All that tells me is that this has happened before. The lab is working on the sample we acquired from Samantha Black's car. Early findings indicate that there is nothing but skin, as if it had been shed."

"Shed? Jesus H. Christ."

"I have an operating theory that it could be a virus of some sort, that the skin being shed is a byproduct of whatever it is," Selena suggested.

"If the skin is shed, then where is the rest of the person?" Ott asked.

"If it's a virus, they could be too ill to show up, or who knows, with the shed skin they may have changed appearance and be unrecognizable."

Ott nodded. "Keep me in the loop on the research, Selena."

"Of course."

Ott left the room, and Selena returned her attention to the century-old photo, trying to see something in it that she wasn't even sure was there.

CHAPTER 3

Simeon White stood on the roof of the skyscraper. He was not alone. In fact, there were several people on the roof with him. White was in his late twenties, but a real go-getter. He had started working for Theory's show five years ago as a production assistant, fetching coffee, making copies—the typical entry level gofer work. Now he was managing the production of segments of the show, a meteoric rise to be sure. One didn't get where he was without stepping on some toes, and kissing some serious ass with the higher- ups, particularly Theory himself. White was good at both, and excellent at his job. He knew what buttons to push almost naturally, with little need for training other than what he could glean empirically.

Simeon stood there, his long dark hair flowing in the wind that seemed stronger higher up than on the street below. Despite the fact that he had jet- black hair, he had a streak of white running through the left side of his mane. Simeon had hollow cheeks, yet chiseled features. White looked at the man, a boy really, even though he was only a few years younger than Simeon.

The boy was dressed in a simple white tunic that flapped in the wind like a sheet drying on a country day. The boy himself was nervous, and Simeon could sense this. He tucked his clipboard under his arm and approached the young man.

"How are you feeling, Thomas?" Simeon asked.

"I...I don't think I can do it," the boy responded, trying to turn away from the ledge of the building.

Simeon grabbed the little prick by the arm. He wouldn't allow him to run off, as the boy clearly yearned to do.

"But it is almost time," White told Thomas.

"What if I miss the mark? I mean, shouldn't there be a stunt man for this or something?" the boy said, peering over the edge of the massive building.

Thomas tried to move away from the edge again, but Simeon White tightened his grip on him.

"Don't be stupid. You know what show this is for, right?"

Thomas looked at the streak in Simeon's hair. He knew what it meant. The boy looked over the edge of the building again.

"I don't see the net," Thomas remarked almost sheepishly.

"Well, of course you don't! We are using a special kind you cannot see. We can't have the cameras pick up on it."

Thomas relaxed a bit, but still peered over the ledge, almost curious.

"Gee, they must spend a lot of money on something like that!" the boy paused, "Mr. White, I don't mean to be difficult, but I was told I would meet him."

Simeon nodded at Thomas.

"Yes, of course; he isn't on set, but I will make sure you get an introduction, and a signed photograph too, some swag—how's that sound?"

"Oh man, that sounds amazing! My parents won't believe it! They have the streak, you know." Thomas said gesturing at his own hair, despite the fact that he didn't bear the homage.

"That is just fantastic, Thomas! They are going to be very, very proud!" Simeon said, clapping the kid on the back. "So, Thomas, are you ready?"

The kid looked down again, staring.

"I guess. I used to jump off a bridge with my friends when I was a kid, but there was water to break the fall," Thomas said.

"Don't look down; trust that the nets will catch you. You are going to be on the Theory Show! It's going to be epic! Think about what your friends and family will say then!"

The boy nodded at Simeon.

"I will give you the cue, and then you jump—OK, Thomas?"

The boy nodded.

"First positions, everyone!" Simeon ordered.

There were several cameramen on the roof who took up a position around Thomas; another operated a drone that hovered nearby. A sound mixer checked the microphone on Thomas to make sure that it was secure and functional. Like worker bees, they were all flying about for the good of the hive. Finally, they all checked in with Simeon White, to let him know it was all systems go.

Simeon saw the trepidation by the boy's body language. He couldn't blame him; it was a long drop, and there were no obvious safety protocols, and that was because there were actually none in place. The boy didn't know that, of course, but perhaps he could sense it somehow.

"Are you ready, Thomas?" Simeon asked

The boy nodded nervously.

"Good, this is going to be great! Mr. Theory is going to be very happy with what you have done for the show. I'm sure he will want to meet you straight away, after he sees the footage."

Thomas looked at Simeon and smiled. "Let's do this!"

"Atta boy! Roll sound! Roll camera!"

"Rolling sound!"

"Rolling camera!"

"Thomas, let me clear the shot, count to five, and go!"

"Got it, Mr. White!"

Simeon moved out of the camera's way and stood watching, counting down himself. But when in his mind he hit five, the boy was still on the roof. White looked around at the crew members shaking their heads. Simeon's face crunched up in certain anger. Finally, he walked up behind the boy and shoved him in the back. Thomas was surprised by this, and tried for a moment to regain his balance. He failed and went off the roof of the skyscraper.

The boy screamed as he fell. Part of him must have known that there were no nets, but what he didn't know was that the people who had put him on this roof and pushed him over it didn't want him to die.

Across from the skyscraper that Thomas jumped off of, and inside another building, was Elysium Theory. He wasn't alone. Next to him stood a young man with a radar gun pointing at the falling boy. Like Simeon White, Eli also had a wisp of white dyed into his otherwise dark hair.

"Is he going to make it?" Theory asked Eli.

"This is trial and error. I have no idea if it will work or not," Eli responded.

Theory looked at his assistant, anger flashing across his face. "I am not interested in theoretical crap, Eli. I need to know how it works!"

"I understand you want answers, sir. I can only tell you what the science is guessing. We have no way of recreating that night; we have no idea what other factors may have been in play."

The radar gun peaked at 75 mph, but the boy splatted on the concrete at the base of the building anyway.

"Not fast enough?" Theory asked.

"We don't know what the ideal velocity is, but it had to be close."

"So, what went wrong?" Theory said, grabbing the radar gun in anger looking at the readings for himself.

"She didn't end up splattered on the concrete, she went somewhere! We WILL get her back. I will get her back! Do you understand me?" Theory said, shaking Eli.

"You want to keep recruiting fans to toss off the building in the name of the show? That is going to catch up with us. At best, they will shut us down, at worst, lock us up and toss the key," Eli protested, shaking himself loose from Theory's grasp.

Theory rubbed his temples. "Yes, of course, you are right. I just... I can't give up. I know she is out there somewhere."

Eli put a hand on his boss' shoulder, in a silly attempt at consolation. The man was inconsolable. He was also insane and murderous, even if the murder was incidental. The loss he had suffered was twisting his head in worse ways than one might expect. Theory was brilliant, but there was a fine line between genius and madness, and clearly the man was dancing well over the madness line of late.

"We need to leave. The authorities will be on site. We need to get you out of here."

"She may come, the other one," Theory said.

"It's not who you think it is. Besides, this isn't an operation in their purview."

Theory thought on it. He knew Eli was right, in his rational mind, but we each have an irrational mind too, and Theory's mind teetered about the border of both. Finally, he let his assistant lead him out the back of the building, away from the splattered boy on the concrete.

CHAPTER 4

Major Ott was the manager of the Center. It housed a great many services of the secret authority. Research, forensics, and training were just some of the things that happened at the well-hidden facility.

From the outside, the place looked like an abandoned home covered in thick foliage, but it also appeared to have serious damage to the roof and side of the house. It was all an illusion. It wasn't a former domicile at all. It was an underground super-complex, the exterior a series of holographic imagery made to be so uninviting that even the most ardent of risk-takers wouldn't dare enter.

Ott had known Selena since childhood. He had come up with her father, and had a pseudo-paternal relationship with the girl, although now she was a woman. Selena had made it through the ranks of the Blacks. She was smart and observant, which made her a great researcher, but she was also a brilliant operative, a role she preferred.

Ott had been with Selena's father when he died. Silas Black had been a formidable man and an operative no enemy wanted to fuck with. He died when Selena was only five; the circumstances were not made public or even available to lower-ranking members of the Black Syndicate. Ott probably wouldn't have been privy himself if he hadn't been there, a fact he had kept hidden from Selena, because at the end of the day if she had asked to know what had happened, paternal Ott would have defied Major Ott and told her. What he told her was that he died with honor, which was true. Silas implored Ott to look after Selena, and he promised he would, but Silas also requested that Selena never be indoctrinated into the syndicate. Ott wasn't able to prevent that from happening. The way the major had figured it, this was for the best. He could keep a closer eye on Selena if she was made to be a Black, something he wouldn't be able to do had she remained a civilian. So, in a twisted way, Major Ott was fulfilling Silas Black's final request.

The Center was equipped with top of the line holographic tech. Unless you knew the place was there, you weren't going to find it. There was an actual structure that the underground complex lived underneath, but even getting to the abandoned farmhouse was laden with holographic countermeasures to deter anyone from advancing on it. In the unlikely event someone did get to the home, it still would be virtually impossible to access the complex underneath. One couldn't find the Blacks; they found you.

The secret organization was government backed. Although it was unclear who actually controlled the syndicate, some said FEMA, some said NSA, some said CIA and FBI. What was clear was that the syndicate known as the Blacks was covert, free to operate with little to no oversight.

Ott sat in his windowless office. They had given him the option of having a faux window that would depict images, like the sea or mountains, perhaps even a golden field, but Ott had declined. He didn't care for the distraction, yet as he stared at his monitor, he was exactly that—distracted.

Ott was logged into all law enforcement channels. Every blip on the radar would cross his desk, and what he saw was a report of a young man, who had either fallen, jumped, or was pushed off a building.

"Fuck," Ott said out loud.

The major furrowed his brow at the report. He was well aware what it meant, although there was little that could be done. He had thought about arresting Theory, keeping him at a Black site so he would be unable to perpetuate the madness. Ott looked at the internal monitor that showed the goings-on inside the compound. There she was, Selena Black, unaware, doing her research. Maybe he would "disappear" Theory. Ott believed that option to be impossible; the conspiracy host had a loyal following. A missing Theory would cause more problems than it solved. Still, it was an appealing thought.

Elysium Theory had exposed the Black Syndicate on more than one occasion, sometimes without even knowing it. There were loads of conspiracy shows, but Theory's show was the most followed and respected. No one had really questioned who the secret operatives were, who came and went almost invisibly before Theory provided visual evidence of their presence at various scenes all over the country, and all over the world. He had put the group, who wanted to remain under the radar, right on the fucking map, exactly where they did not want to be. Yet nothing was said, and nothing was done to counteract Theory, the thought being that if they were to respond or react, that would indicate that he was right about something. Still, the message boards dedicated to these things had been made more aware, and now even reported sightings of Black operatives, whereas before they did not.

Ott accessed the CC feeds from the area where the young man had been found at the building. He was looking to catch Theory coming out of that very building, so he could pick him up for questioning. It wasn't the first time someone had met an untimely end from that particular building; the time of night was similar to the others who had met that fate. There had been men and women, but all had been approximately the same height and weight.

"Got you, little bugger!" Ott said to the closed-circuit feed.

It wasn't the big fish, it was a little fish. It was that shit bird production manager, Simeon White, practically sashaying out of the building. Ott thought he could snatch him up and get him to implicate his boss. The major picked up his office phone and called it in. He thought of letting Selena interrogate White; she was very good at getting answers. After he ordered White picked up, he looked at the monitor that showed the research lab that Selena was working in. It was empty. Ott squinted his eyes in disbelief.

"Shit!" Ott said to himself.

The major looked at the lab where Selena was working, expecting her to materialize. She didn't. He clicked about the other video feeds that monitored the interior of the compound. There was no sign of Selena. Still, it meant nothing. She could be in a section of the place that wasn't under observation.

A bead of sweat formed on the major's forehead and dripped down his face. He took a deep breath and sat in his chair, then realized one way he could both control and not control the situation at the same time. It was risky, but the fire was lit, why not play with it?

He picked up the phone. "Please send Selena to my office."

CHAPTER 5

Theory skulked into his apartment. He was so intent on getting to some drugs and alcohol that he didn't realize that the door to his flat didn't close all the way. That was how desperate his sadness was, bordering on the truly pathetic. All Theory wanted was to numb the pain, forget the loss. Of course, the pain would be worse, a thousand times so when he sobered up, but Theory didn't care. He needed to stop the relentless pain, if even for a little while.

Theory was focused on finding his stash of cocaine, not that he could remember if he had finished it all (he had; he always did.) The man with the shock of white hair was losing his mind, in more ways than one, truth be told. The desperation not to feel created a tornado of a man. Theory was looking everywhere for some of his hidden stash that didn't exist. Finally, after tossing cushions, ripping books form his shelves, even looking in the safe, he settled on chugging down some vodka. It burned his throat, and that made him hate himself for needing it, but the hatred dissipated when the liquor kicked in.

Theory wasn't done. He picked up the phone and made a call. "Can you send the same? And have her bring what she did last time?"

Theory hung up the phone. He guzzled more booze, plopped on the sofa, and simply stared out into the night cityscape.

The woman didn't bother to knock. She actually had thought that the door had been left ajar on purpose, as part of the fantasy. She had to make sure the wig was properly affixed just in case he wanted to get physical this time, even though on most occasions he didn't want sex. She pushed the door open.

"Hi!" she said as enthusiastically as possible.

Theory stirred from the couch, vaguely looking up, forgetting briefly that he had called for this person. She looked great, and he immediately perked up as soon as he laid eyes on her. It wasn't her, Theory knew that, but she looked like her, and he could pretend that it was.

"Hi," Theory mustered almost desperately.

The woman with the shoulder-length black hair, a kiss of white running through it, smiled seductively. She straddled Theory and rubbed on his growing cock through his pants.

"I like that," he managed to say.

The woman wore tight tank top with no bra. She was sex on a stick; her nipples were poking through the thin, soft fabric; perfect perky breasts were seen in outline. She wore form-fitting tight jeans, clad in all black other than the simple streak of white that ran through her hair. The woman pulled a long vial from her tank top and shook it in front of Theory.

"You asked for some of this?" she asked him.

Theory snatched the vial from her, almost maniacally, absolutely with desperation. This was the mind-numbing agent trifecta: coke, booze, and sex.

"Let me help," the woman suggested, taking the vial from Theory.

She took off her top, unveiling perfectly shaped breasts. She lay down, simultaneously unscrewing the top of the container and expertly putting the powder in between her tits. Theory's eyes lit up as he swooped in and collected the powder through his nose. He came back up, almost for air, except he was ingesting euphoria.

"Fuck, that's good!"

Theory chased the nose candy with a swig of vodka and then handed the bottle to his companion. She put it on the table and had a snort of coke for herself. She put the vial down and ran her hands over Theory's crotch through the pants, slowly. The woman smiled at her power to make men's cocks grow almost instantly, but particularly Theory's.

"I belong to you," she uttered, stroking him as she said it.

Theory became turgid quickly and she unzipped his pants and took him in her mouth. It didn't take long. The fantasy of whatever role she was playing always got him off, despite the drugs and alcohol that should have slowed him. He exploded in her mouth, which she normally didn't allow, but he paid well, and he didn't expect her to drink it down. She went to the bathroom, spit it out, and used half a tube of toothpaste to get the taste of him gone, although it never really was.

When she came back, she didn't see Theory. She wasn't sure what to do at this point. This guy always paid top dollar for the drugs, and her services, role-playing included. He had more time on the clock, so she sat on the couch. The woman looked at the cocaine, contemplating a bump; maybe if she were spending the entire night, like most of the high-end coke heads wanted, she would, but this guy never asked for that. This guy never even wanted to fuck. This guy wanted a woman in a wig, some words, and a blowie. Usually after blowing his wad, he just sat on the couch numbing his unbending pain; this was the first time he was unaccounted for. She hemmed and hawed as to what to do, until finally she heard sobbing. The woman followed the sound to the balcony.

Theory was balled up in a corner, trusty vodka bottle by his side. He was crying. The woman empathized with him. Often her job encompassed lonely men; not that one would think it, but she actually spent more time just being a good listener or companion rather than a sex toy. The woman empathized; maybe it was just about control. Regardless, she leaned down to Theory and touched his face.

"Why don't you come inside? I can stay longer, we can talk more."

Theory looked up at the woman. Something had changed. There was a wisp of blonde hair poking out from under her wig. Theory stared at the errant hairs.

"You aren't her!" he said, agitated.

The woman was frightened. Theory was clearly upset. He pointed at her in an accusatory manner. She backed up, away from the oncoming lunatic of a man.

"You're an imposter!" he yelled.

"No, I belong to you!" she attempted.

"No, no, no! You don't get to say that!" Theory ripped off the wig.

Theory looked incredulously at the jet-black fake hair with the streak of white in it. The woman backed slowly away, hoping to run into the door, but she tripped over some furniture and fell backwards. She looked up at the wild-eyed man coming at her.

"Please, I'm just an escort!"

"Are you from the other world?" Theory asked. "You are, aren't you."

The woman shook her head. "What? No."

She managed to scramble to her feet. She turned away and ran for the door, but he caught her by the hair and threw her against the wall. He sniffed at her as if to detect some otherworld stench on her.

"Go back to your world and tell them to give her back to me!" he said, releasing her.

The woman opened the door and ran down the hallway, scared for her life. She didn't turn back, despite the fact that she had left her purse and her wig. He hadn't even paid her.

CHAPTER 6

The production offices of the show hadn't been active. The show itself had been in reruns, while the notorious host was on a break for "personal" reasons. Oddly, the show seemed to maintain its cachet, mostly due to Simeon White. He prodded conversation on the message boards that Theory himself was wrapped up in something nefarious, which in part was of course true.

Simeon was one of two people in the office. Eli was the other. The two men didn't care for each other; both were in competition to be Theory's favorite pet. Both thought that they were in line to take over the show should Theory retire or nose dive straight into the deep end. There had never been any indication that Theory would retire or be forced to, let alone that one of them would take over as the frontline act of the show. Still, they both hung on to that notion.

Despite the men being in the same place at the same time, they weren't even close to each other. Simeon was in his office sorting mail. People would send things in to the show, mostly nothing of importance like things to be signed, requests for Theory to show up at a fan's birthday party, or some other bullshit. But Simeon was looking for leads. Evidence of something worth putting on air. Stepping into Theory's shoes was a long shot, but Simeon knew that if he were to succeed at his goals, he had to be willing to do about just about anything.

Eli wasn't one to get his hands dirty. Simeon thought he was no more than a daddy's girl. He rarely left Theory's side. It was a wonder Eli was in the office without his master, unless Theory had set him on some task of lunacy. Simeon looked at Eli, who was sitting in Theory's office, at his desk, like the proud pet that he was.

Eli was barely aware of Simeon. He knew he was there but could not have cared less. Undoubtedly, he was bottom-feeding from the mail bag to pitch something worse than idiotic that would never make the light of day. Eli admired Simeon for his willingness to do just about anything, but chastised him for never getting the results he so desperately craved.

Eli saw himself as more noble than Simeon, despite being younger by two years and having less tenure. Eli thought himself indispensable, and for all intents and purposes he was, but the same could said about Simeon. These two were the lifeblood of the show, particularly since Theory had gone even deeper off the deep end.

Eli sat at his boss' desk and watched the footage of the experiment. It was brutal even by Theory's standards. Eli's boss was more interested in seeing what happened when a person was dropped off the same building over and over again, than in actually doing his show. This was the third splat out of three. No one was sure what the renowned conspiracy host was after, but it was getting bad. He seemed insistent on dropping people off the same building over and over until whatever he was looking to happen, happened.

Eli wondered how long the host could keep this up without getting caught. Eli assumed that if it ended badly for Theory, the show would suffer, and Eli wouldn't get the chance he was after, a shot at becoming the host himself. Of course, he knew he wasn't the only one in line for the job; Simeon was after it too, and he had been with the show longer, but Eli knew that Theory favored him, as he should. Eli busted his ass for Elysium Theory, even helping his murderous experiments.

An email notice came across the screen. It was into Theory's account. Eli answered the embattled star's emails, too. He was sure Theory didn't bother to even monitor it himself. Eli stopped watching the death fall and went into the email. It was from an unknown address, directed at the show, but attention to Theory. The odd thing was that the return address was unlike any Eli had ever seen before. It contained symbols, sort of like Asian characters, except these were unlike anything Eli had ever seen, almost otherworldly. There was an attachment. Eli clicked on it. Normally he wouldn't have, but the office computers were equipped with military-grade antivirals. If it were something nefarious, the system would catch it.

The attachment was a grainy video message. Eli squinted to try and make out the man in the video. He seemed to have raven-black hair and was dressed in all black. Wherever he was being filmed was utterly nondescript and was so grainy it could be anywhere. What was clear was that the man was distressed. The audio was in and out, and was even worse than the picture quality.

"... War IS coming!" the man in the video said, *right before all the power went out.*

"Shit" Eli said to himself

The emergency lights went on. But there was something else—voices. Eli knew something was off. It was too late at night for anyone else to be in the building, let alone audible from the production office on the 12th floor. Then he saw lights that seemed attached to the voices. Eli hid under Theory's desk and peered out to try and see what was happening.

Simeon wasn't as lucky or as smart as Eli. He didn't bother to hide, so he saw the Black Syndicate insertion team come in like the paramilitary professionals that they were. They all had night vision goggles, and assault rifles, except one, a woman.

The team quickly identified their target. The six men in black moved on Simeon with precision. Simeon didn't move. The men in black all had their assault rifles pointed at him.

"Guys, is that really necessary?

Selena moved between her men to face Simeon. She gestured for them to lower their weapons, and they did.

"You alone?" she asked.

Simeon's eyes flitted briefly toward Eli. "What does it look like?"

Selena nodded. "I don't want to restrain you. Come with us to answer some questions, and I won't."

Eli watched as Simeon walked out with the Black Syndicate. He waited for what seemed like an hour, although it probably wasn't even close to that long. The lights to the office were restored, and Eli came out from under the desk. Eli went to leave but remembered the grainy message in Theory's email.

Eli rebooted the computer and forwarded the email to his own account, then got the hell out of there.

CHAPTER 7

Simeon White was seated in the interrogation room. His feet were shackled to the floor, but his upper body was free, sort of. They had him hooked up to what he guessed was a lie detector test of some sort. He had a blood pressure cuff on his arm, two tubes around his chest and various other spots on his hands, and forehead that had sticky pads attached to wires running into the silver table that was in front of him. The lights in the room were very bright, almost hot. Simeon was sweating as he stared at the blackness of the artificially darkened window that the two-way glass provided.

Simeon White knew that he had been taken by the Blacks. This was trouble that even he knew he might not be able to get himself out of. He tried to remain calm. Simeon was a high-energy, high-anxiety sort of guy. It could work for him in some senses, but he had made a point of trying to learn calming techniques to help him manage when he was over the top. He closed his eyes and tried to mediate, but that other person that lives in all of us, who predicts nothing but disaster, would not let him rest.

Simeon was distracted by the sound of the lone door opening. He opened his eyes to see Selena enter. Two armed men started to enter with her, but she waved them off and they backed out of the room. Selena wasn't armed; it wasn't necessary, Simeon was a producer on a conspiracy show, not exactly a hardened criminal.

"You," Simeon said.

Selena looked at Simeon with curiosity.

"Me, what?" she asked him.

"You look just like her." Simeon told her.

"Like who?"

"You don't know?"

Selena squinted her eyes at Simeon. "How do you know she and I aren't the same?"

Simeon thought about it. Perhaps his mind was playing tricks on him. Yet he was sure, it was her, yet definitely not her.

"Why am I shackled?" Simeon asked.

"It's for your own safety, Mr. White."

"And what do I call you? I mean besides Ms. Black?"

"Right now, I am your interrogator, Mr. White; that's what you can call me."

"Why am I being interrogated?"

"I think we both know the answer to that."

"If I did, I doubt I would ask."

"Your boss, Mr. White. He seems to have a fascination with people falling off a certain building. I'd like to know why."

"Theory has a lot of fascinations. I am not privy to the rationale behind them. But if you are interested in Theory, why am I here?"

Selena moved toward Simeon. She put her hands on the table and looked at her prisoner. "You know who we are, obviously. I am sure you have a sense of what we are capable of, right?"

Simeon nodded. "You *do* realize I work on a conspiracy show? We hear things about you guys all the time, but it is rare that we can validate."

"I'm sure you will see the benefit of cooperating."

"I am happy to help, but you are asking me about the ideation of another person—how could I possibly know that?"

Selena nodded. "It is a fair point, Mr. White. Simeon Adam White— the Simeon is a family name isn't it? It's from your maternal grandfather, right? You are a producer of the Elysium Theory Program. Born in New Orleans and raised by your mother, Judy, who died last year from ovarian cancer. *Condolences.* Graduated from Tulane University with a degree in occult studies. You moved to the big city after you graduated and slithered your way into a paid internship on the Theory show, where you worked your way up to the job you hold today, a real self-starter. I even have it on good authority that you started this bit of symbolic hokum."

Selena flicked the white dyed strand of hair that cascaded off Simeon's face. He smiled at her, and then he started clapping.

"Very good, Selena; you have done your homework."

Selena cocked her head at Simeon. He sniggered.

"Selena Ursula Black, you are the first woman to successfully complete SEAL training. I understand you also served several tours, too, but that was classified, so I had problems confirming it. I do know that you moved to operations, because you have a fascination with stratagem, which led you to the post you now hold, although I cannot say what that post is, or with any certainty confirm that you or the organization exists today. You are a ghost—beyond one, actually. Yet you stand here in front of me, where I can see with my own eyes that you are indeed real."

Selena backed up off the table, without taking her eyes off him. "I'm impressed. That information is under lock and key. How did you get it?"

"I can't reveal my sources—journalistic integrity, and whatnot."

Selena laughed, "Integrity? *Good one.* You realize I have the power to hold you indefinitely in a black site, until no one remembers that you existed at all. Total erasure."

"It's not necessary to threaten me. Perhaps I can help."

"I'm listening."

"It seems to me that you aren't interested in me; you just want to use me to get to Theory."

"He has been a thorn in our side for years, although I'm not sure how aware of it he actually is."

"Elysium has gone off the deep end. He is trying to find answers to questions that may not even exist."

"That's why he is tossing people off that building?"

Simeon nodded. "But you can't prove it, can you? Looks like a suicide?"

"I wish I could say I was surprised you knew."

"I am a good producer, even of rudimentary physics experiments."

"Physics?"

"I will make a deal to give him up, but I get immunity and a wide berth to operate the show once Theory is gone."

"You are a little weasel."

"Is that a yes?"

"I will let you know," Selena said

Selena Black exited the interrogation room. Simeon White sniggered a bit, oddly relaxed for someone in chains.

CHAPTER 8

Theory stood, eyes closed, conducting an imaginary orchestra from his balcony. It was as if he were a blind man, yet at the same time, he could see another dimension where the music that he orchestrated played. It was both beautiful and disturbing all at once. Beautifully disturbing, or was it disturbingly beautiful?

The door to his flat was still ajar from when the escort left. Eli looked at the open door with trepidation. He thought about turning around and leaving, but after Simeon being arrested at the office, he needed guidance. He knew that Theory was likely on one of his benders; he always was, after another failure.

"Hello?" Eli said gingerly, pushing the door open further.

The place was a mess. There were two vodka bottles, each still with a minuscule amount of booze still inside. A vial of white powder kept the bottles company. Eli could hear humming coming from the balcony.

"Elysium?"

Eli entered carefully. Theory had been going down a steady road of instability and probably insanity. Losing her had warped his mind, and trying to compensate with drugs and alcohol wasn't helping him untangle his addled mind.

Theory was home, but he wasn't really there. The drugs and alcohol allowed him passage out of the world he was in, and into the one where she was. The libations had limbered up his mind at the cost of his soul. He didn't care; he would hurl himself off that building if it meant he could be with her. For a brief moment, he was with her. Even as it looked from the outside like he was conducting an unseen orchestra, in his mind's eye he was stroking her face, her hair, the curve of her breasts.

Eli moved onto the balcony, not knowing what to do.

"Theory?"

The white-haired man acted as if he were in another place and time. Eli looked at him, utterly flummoxed as to what to do.

"Theory!"

There was nothing, no response. Eli was just an executive assistant. His boss had been acting more and more erratic of late. Any sane employee would have left for greener pastures, but Eli, much like Simeon, figured he might be the next in line to ascend the throne. Plus, he had put in almost six years with the man. Granted, for the most part he was an asshole, but this was Elysium Theory! Theory started just by running a website devoted to unearthing conspiracies, but then graduated to a bigger stage of radio, television, then streaming, becoming more outlandish as he became more successful.

His ideas were not always well received, and he found himself at the center of many controversies. The most famous included that the US government was staging false flag terrorist attacks, the moon landing was shot by Stanley Kubrick on a Sound stage in London, and the crème de la crème, that the Newtown Elementary School shootings didn't actually happen. Theory's biggest push was about the New World Order, which postulated that government and big business conspired to manipulate the populace, eventually corralling us all inside to be worker drones from our homes, where we could be monitored and controlled more easily.

Theory's fans gobbled all of it up. The more he pissed people off, the more the Theorists loved him, even going so far as to dye a wisp of their hair white in homage. In the six years that Eli had been with him, it seemed that Theory's level of asshole activity grew exponentially with each success, as the host became more and more audacious. It all had gone to his head, and then *he lost her.* After that, he spiraled out of control on an entirely different level. Sure, before that he had been arrested a few times for protesting, some bullshit charges—operating a megaphone without a permit, and disorderly conduct. Things clearly degenerated from there. This fuck of a man had become murderous, although perhaps not intentionally, but the last young man was the third person to nosedive off that same building at the same time of night. The Black Syndicate was involved. Something had to be done.

Eli placed a hand on Theory's shoulder gently, so he could wake him from whatever trance he had imbibed himself into. The man practically jumped out of his skin.

"NO! Never do that! I was with her..." Theory yelled at his unsuspecting assistant, pushing him back.

"I wouldn't have bothered you, but...."

"But what? You are always bothering me, you annoying little turd."

Theory walked back into the apartment. He moved to the coffee table, emptied the vial of powder onto it, and took a heavy snort. There was some powder residue on the tip of his nose. His eyes blackened as if he were devoid of any emotion, and then he took a swig of what was left in one of the vodka bottles. He plopped almost satisfactorily on the couch and looked at Eli, who had followed him back inside.

"I don't want to be alone tonight," Theory stated, matter-of-factly.

"You aren't alone, Elysium. I'm here."

"You know what I mean. Eli, I want you to get me some women."

"Yeah, well, that can be an issue. They don't want to come back here after the abuse you put them through."

"So, call some hookers. I like them better anyway."

"Who do you think I was talking about? At least they get compensated. I'm afraid that's the best you can do right now. But there is a problem at the office."

Theory face-planted into the coke again. "So what? There are always problems at the office. This is what I have you for, so I don't have to deal with the shit."

"This one1 is above my pay grade."

Theory looked at him, finally telling him, "Spit it out, Eli."

Eli took a deep breath. "The Blacks raided the office. They took Simeon, amongst other things, like computers."

Theory laughed. "Those pricks have been after me for decades. Simeon is a good soldier; he won't tell them anything."

"You have to stop with the experiments. She isn't coming back, and if you don't stop, you are going to get snatched yourself."

"Eli, I want you to get me some women for the night, and then I want you to get out."

Eli looked at his boss in disbelief, although he really should not have been surprised at all. Theory finished the remainder of the white powder and then guzzled what was left in the second vodka bottle.

"You know what? Go down to the store and get me a couple more bottles of this," Theory said, holding the container aloft.

"I don't think that's a good idea."

"I don't pay you to think, Eli. One day my empire could be yours. All I ask is that you do what I want while I am still kicking. After, you can think as much or as little as you wish."

Could. Fucking prick. Eli nodded and left the flat to do his boss' bidding.

CHAPTER 9

Simeon had been sitting in the chains for a long period of time. He meditated as best he could in order to disallow the anxiety to take over just like she wanted it. He had no clue how long he had been sitting in the sterile room. It felt like the other side of forever.

Selena Black came through the door, finally. She had a plate of fruit and a liter of water. Simeon stood like a trained animal, waiting for his daily feeding.

"You must be hungry," Selena said, standing at a distance.

Simeon licked his lips and nodded.

"So, we just need to come to an understanding, yes?"

"Sure, Selena."

"I will let you go, but from now on you work for me. I am going to nail your boss for whatever he has been up to at that building. You will testify, in a Black Court. It won't be public, of course, and Theory will go away, leaving you to ascend the throne."

Simeon's slippery smile sent shock waves through his entire system, maybe even Selena's as well.

"I thought you would like that deal."

"Oh, I do. Very much so. Now may I be free and have some food and water?"

"Sure," Selena said, not moving.

"Now would work for me."

Selena nodded. "We will just need you to sign away your soul first."

Simeon's smile sunk like a downed ship.

Selena waved her hand in the air and the door opened again. Two men draped in the paramilitary black uniform that mirrored Selena's entered. One took the food and water from Selena and handed her a manila folder and a pen. Selena opened the folder and reviewed the documents. Finally, she moved to Simeon and she placed the opened folder in front of him. His eyes widened a bit as he read.

"This says I will be sentenced for life for failure to testify against Theory—now why would I sign off on that?"

"Because you are a highly motivated little shit, Simeon, that's why. We want to guarantee ourselves a caught big fish, and you can be the little one that swims away uneaten."

"You didn't mention this before."

"It's mentioned now; what's the problem? You give me what I want and it's a non-issue."

"I feel like I have no choice in the matter."

"Well, you choose not to sign it, and let him get away with whatever he is trying to accomplish, and no one will be bothered by your presence in the known world ever again. You can choose simply to rot away in one of our secret prisons, in solitary confinement."

Simeon stared at her incredulously. Selena handed him the pen, and Simeon signed away his soul—what little there was left to sell.

"I thought you would agree," Selena said, smiling at her success. She motioned to the man holding the plate and water.

The man put the plate in front of Simeon, who was ravenous. He devoured the slices of apple and orange; the water came next, as he drank about half in one gulp.

"He won't need the chains anymore, either."

The other man unchained the prisoner, who kept eating as if being freed were almost insignificant. The door opened again. Simeon looked up, seeing Major Ott. The burly man looked troubled. Selena regarded the man.

"I will be right out," Selena told her superior.

The man didn't move. Selena shifted her eyes back to Simeon. "We aren't done here. I will be back."

Simeon watched as Selena left with the man. He vaguely heard what Ott said to Selena, something along the lines of, "It's happened again."

CHAPTER 10

The body, if you could call it that, was draped over the chair like a worn coat discarded after a long day. It was as if someone had taken off a skin suit and left it behind. Men in black scoured the scene looking for answers that simply didn't exist.

Selena came into the room and stared incredulously at whatever was left of Samuel Black. The former member of the syndicate had been long since retired. Selena hadn't known him, but she had known of him. He had a reputation of being a serious asshole. He was one of those ultra-entitled law enforcement types—the kind of bullshit that comes with time, and getting away with lord knows what professionally.

Still, Samuel Black lived a very simple third act, aside from the way he checked out, of course. If one had stepped into this person's home, one would see an aged pack rat, who had outlived most his contemporaries, and had become resigned to the fact that he would be discovered days, maybe even weeks after his death. Given the state of what was left of him, how long he had been there was up to heavy debate that would be answered eventually by the crack forensic team that was on site trying to determine how to get the remains into a body bag without losing even more of its integrity.

Selena stood next to the forensic team. They had a gurney with a body bag on it, yet seemed confounded as to how to get what looked like shedded skin into it.

"Any initial ideas?" Selena asked the team leader.

The man looked at her with raised eyebrows. "Not a fucking clue. I've never seen anything like this."

"I have, in research."

"Really? What had happened?"

"No one knows—it was just photographed. I didn't have a forensic report; I just found a photo in the files."

"This has happened before? Where?"

"Germany."

"So, we can conference with our offices over there."

"We could, except they didn't see it first-hand."

"How is that possible?"

"It was recorded in 1933, by accident, and definitely not by one of us."

"You are telling me that whatever this is has been happening for at least 100 years?"

"It seems so, but I need you to tell me what you can, as soon as possible."

"I'm sure, but we have to find a way to take the subject without it contaminating the body—or what's left of it."

Both watched as the two men in hazmat suits tried to scoop the flat skin with a two flat metal pieces. They were having little success. Selena pulled up the image on her tablet—it was a harrowing sight, of a human sleeve of skin draped over a headstone in a cemetery. The headstone had initials S.B. on it. The team leader looked at the image.

"Huh, that can't be coincidence."

"What do you mean?" Selena asked.

"S.B? Can you zoom in on the stone?"

Selena zoomed in and the headstone was enlarged. They looked at it closely.

"You see it?" he asked her.

"I can barely make it out, but it's definitely there," Selena said, tracing a hand logo that indented the headstone, just like the ones that were on all the black uniforms. You wouldn't really know they were there unless you were a member of the covert agency.

"So, someone has been hunting us for at least 100 years."

"Someone—or something." she responded.

They watched as the hazmat-clad people managed to slide what was left of Samuel Black into the body bag.

"I need all your resources on this," she instructed.

The man nodded and followed the body bag out of the secluded domicile. Selena scanned Samuel Black's house. Aside from some photos from years past, one would be hard put to have a remote understanding of who lived in the space, other than a pack rat. Clutter. That was the interesting part of it; if someone or something came and sucked out all the insides of this old man wouldn't there have been a struggle? The stacks of books, and boxes, and whatever had a look of controlled chaos. Books, magazines, even newspapers from lord knows how long ago were stacked consciously almost to the ceilings, coated with unmolested dust. *There is no way someone did this. But what happened? And how did the same thing happen in Germany a century prior?*

One of Selena's men approached. He was documenting the scene with a tablet. Selena pondered what she saw of the room. "You find anything?"

"It's curious," the man began. "Nothing seems out of order, no sign of struggle—then I switched to infrared, and now look."

"What the fuck?"

Selena stared at the screen incredulously. She saw what appeared to be powder-blue hand- and footprints leading up to the chair, on the mouth of the skin, and walking up to the mirror that was on the wall, a big splotch was in the center of the glass.

"Yep, what the fuck indeed," the man repeated.

"The hand and footprints look humanoid," she said.

"That's true, but whatever it was hardly could be human. May walk like one, and enter like one, but it looks like it exited through the mirror."

"Let's have a look behind the mirror. There must be something."

The man directed another to help him lower the mirror from the wall. There was nothing behind it.

"We will need to run some tests on the mirror. Make sure it gets preserved, and quarantine the property. I'm guessing we will be studying it for a long time."

The man nodded and Selena left, a head full of the unknown and wild imaginings.

CHAPTER 11

Eli lived in a shitty part of town. Although he made good money as Theory's right-hand man, he never spent much of it; there was some part of him that made him believe that all good things end prematurely. The job and the pay were both very good—the treatment, not so much. Although he had worked for Theory for several years in different capacities, it was clear that his boss was becoming unhinged. Loss will do that, but other people seemed to have a less reckless way of grieving. Truth be told, one had to be a little nuts to do this kind of work. There had to be an open-mindedness, but with that often came a touch of crazy that made that level of acceptance possible for the conspiracy theory set.

The apartment was dilapidated and small. Paint was flaking off the wall on one side like dandruff, while the other side sweated with moisture from a leak or broken pipes in the walls. There wasn't even a stove, just a hot plate with a worn can used to heat coffee or soup. Eli pulled the sad string that lit a partially cracked lightbulb, which was the sole light source for the small room. There was a beat-up twin mattress that looked as if it had been found in a dumpster; a sad, thin blanket with several holes in it lay strewn across the mattress. The only other furniture was a small round desk and a single chair that didn't match. Eli placed on the table the one thing of real value he possessed: a tablet.

The one thing Eli needed more than to re-watch the bizarre message he pilfered from Theory's email was to have a drink. Eli wasn't much of a drinker, but some days simply called for a stiff belt of numbness that only a strong libation could provide. Eli needed to get his bearings, quantify another death he had on his conscience. A stronger man would have stopped his homicidal boss, but Eli didn't see what Theory was doing as murder. He was experimenting, and his motivation was love, and Eli's motivation was possibly to take over the show when Theory retired, or perhaps got jammed up for his "experiments." Of course, Eli realized that he wasn't the only one in the running. Simeon White had made a name for himself as well, even branding out the white streak that dedicated fans as well as crew had dyed into their hair as a sign of fealty. It was amazing how the concept had taken off. Eli admired Simeon but despised him at the same time. They didn't get along, due mostly to the fact that they were both in line to take over the show, and both had tasted the thrill of on-air reporting. It hadn't been verbalized per se, but Theory had set up the internal competition for who would succeed him. Eli wondered if Simeon had been eliminated from the unofficial competition thanks to the Black Syndicate. He also wondered if they would be after him next. Eli and Simeon were not only vying for the head spot, but they had been Theory's top lieutenants for a while now—their value to the Blacks, if they were after Elysium, would be high.

Eli poured some homemade bathtub gin from a mason jar into a glass. He had learned the trade from his grandmother, who in turn had learned the recipe from her relatives who had to survive Prohibition, from a financial standpoint, but also an alcoholic one. He was very careful about what he consumed—one drink, maybe once every ten days. The batches were strong, so he didn't need much. Eli took a healthy sip from the glass. He almost felt relief as the booze singed his throat and warmed his entire soul.

"Shit," he said, looking at the tablet that sat on his table, almost inviting him further down the rabbit hole.

Eli drank the rest of the liquor in one gulp, wincing as it burned him with a warm, wicked embrace. He placed the empty glass in the sink, went to the tablet, and pulled up his email. His haste to send it to himself when the Blacks infiltrated the production office left Eli uncertain whether he had succeeded in forwarding it, but he had.

Eli watched the grainy video again. It wasn't much more informative than the first viewing. It was as if the black-haired man, dressed in all black, had been captured through a filter that deliberately made him hard to see; yet there was something very familiar about him. It was odd, to be sure, especially the part where the man said that there was a war on the horizon. *Perhaps it was some old footage from the past—that would explain a lot.* Eli's thought made sense, but at the same time didn't seem right. He watched the video again, and then something strange happened. There was a knock at the door.

No one ever knocked on the door. Eli ignored it, until the knock came again.

"I know you are in there. I can hear you," the voice in the hall bellowed.

Much like the video, the familiar voice that he heard was there, yet it didn't make sense. Eli got up and answered the door so he could see for himself. It was as he had thought—Simeon was standing there, and he had a bottle of scotch with him.

"Aren't you going to invite me in?"

Eli stood bewildered for a moment, and then stepped aside. "How did you find me?"

"Oh please, is that a real question? Is there another chair?" Simeon asked incredulously.

"What do you want?"

"To get hammered with a friend."

"Is that a real sentiment?"

"Fine—to get hammered with a colleague."

"And there it is. What happened to you? I saw you get snatched up."

"I did what I always do, Eli. I talked my way out of it."

"You talked your way of the Black Syndicate? Even for you, that seems like a tall task."

Simeon looked around the flat. The disdain on his face was evident. He unscrewed the bottle of Scotch. Simeon contemplated asking for a glass, but then decided against it and took a heathy swig. It was smooth, aged liquor and it went down very well. He passed the bottle to Eli before answering. "They are going after him."

Eli grabbed the bottle and took a small swig, and as he did he knew he would never taste something this fancy ever again. He tried to savor the moment but was distracted by the notion that it appeared that his boss was going to be fucked, and not in the good way. "What does that mean?"

"It means that they have had Theory on their radar since he started spitting vitriol on his show twenty years ago. We know he is full of shit, but chances are he hit on something without knowing it, and whatever that is, has sensitivities to the Black Syndicate. This business with the tests at the building is just giving them the license they need to erase him once and for all."

"Shit. I have to warn him!" Eli said, handing the bottle back.

Simeon looked at Eli. "We aren't warning anyone. Even if we did, you and I both know he wouldn't listen. Theory is gunna do Theory—he always has, and that's not changing, especially when he is riding the bullet train to crazy town."

Eli nodded, knowing full well Simeon was right. He took another smooth pull from the bottle. Turned out Simeon was right about a lot of things. "What about the show?"

"We run it. It isn't as if we don't have the experience. We have been doing it for years between us anyway."

Eli nodded, but this was odd even for Simeon. Perhaps Theory had only used the unofficial competition to be the face, heart, and soul of the show to motivate them to work harder for him. Simeon was correct in the notion that they were more than capable of handling the duties that came with the program; they both had done on-air segments, and there was no reason they both couldn't propel the next incarnation of the show. The strange part was that Simeon suddenly wanted to share in the endeavor. Eli took another glorious pull from the bottle. It somehow seemed smoother the more one drank. He passed the bottle back to Simeon. "So now what?"

"We wait, we keep producing our own segments, and when the time comes, we go the executives and tell them they can have their top-rated show back, with you and me starring."

"What about him?"

"Theory? Eli, he is a dead man walking. Once they snatch him—and they *will* snatch him—we take over, permanently."

"A coup? I have never seen myself doing something like that."

"It's not a coup. We care about the show, and we have the skill set to take over from someone whose time has run out. The Black Syndicate is just sorta helping with the process."

Simeon drank and passed the bottle back to Eli. Eli took the bottle with certain enthusiasm. Simeon knew he had him right where he wanted him. Eli took another pull from the bottle. He was drunk, and he knew it; so did Simeon. He leaned closer to Eli, and not surprisingly, Eli didn't move away from him, so Simeon pushed into Eli closer, touching his leg and seeing a bulge grow in his pants. Simeon seductively touched Eli's cock on the outside of his jeans. He had grown hard quickly.

"Why don't we go to my place? I think you will find it very comfortable," Simeon said before locking lips with Eli.

Simeon was bisexual, or at least he used his sexuality to get what he wanted out of both genders. Truth was that Simeon liked to keep people at a safe distance, and often he equated sexual intimacy with real intimacy. Eli's reasoning was different; he tended to accept any advances on him, although he hadn't had any experiences with men. He didn't care. Eli battled feelings of being unwanted. It was deep rooted, from his time of bouncing from foster care to foster care. He still didn't believe anyone wanted him for good, but sex made him feel like he was desired, at least for a little while.

"You don't like my place?"

Simeon wore a confused look. For a change, he didn't know what to say.

"I'm just yanking your chain. This place is a shit hole; even the cockroaches won't fuck in here."

"You had me for a second there. Let's get outta here."

CHAPTER 12

The sun was rising, but Theory couldn't even get it up. At this point he was on his third woman, and he had lost track of the drugs and booze; he was on too much of each to give a fuck.

The woman between his legs was frustrated. She didn't want to be there anymore; she felt almost like a captive. Truth was, she was a little afraid, and she had reason to be. It wasn't her first time at his flat, although the more often she visited, the more fucked up he seemed to be, and sometimes violent. She had told herself she wouldn't come back after the last time, but she always told herself that; besides, her agency said she was one of only a few women who could do what he wanted, except the last time she didn't get the routine quite right and he grabbed her. He had promised that he wouldn't do it again, but she could sense his frustration building, and he was so messed up from partying all night. She continued to slurp at his flaccid cock, looking up in the hopes that he would give up on trying to come, but he just sat there, eyes closed, imagining lord knows what.

Finally, she just stopped. Theory groaned and struggled to raise his head to see what had happened.

The woman became more uncomfortable, if that were possible. She wiped her mouth of the saliva and got off her knees for the first time in what seemed like hours.

Theory got himself up and grabbing a bottle that had nothing in it, trying to guzzle some. "Who said you should stop?"

The woman looked at him incredulously. "I've been sucking your dick for an hour—what more do you want?"

"To suck it for another hour!"

The woman was nervous. She stood up suddenly and lost her balance a bit on the coffee table. She managed to catch herself, but so did Theory. He had surprised her and gotten up off the couch quicker than she could imagine in his state. He grabbed her by the hair—the wig really, the one all the girls he ordered were mandated to wear. She pulled away faster now. This time, she tripped over the coffee table, her blonde hair spilling out as she hit the ground hard, leaving Theory more enraged, holding the raven-black wig with the white streak through it.

"Who are you?" Theory demanded, "Impostor!"

The woman scrambled to her feet, limped her way to the door, and unlocked it as fast as she could. Theory chased her, but between the drugs and alcohol he wasn't much of a pursuer, other than to scare the woman out the flat and away for good, leaving her wig and purse behind.

"Fucking spy! You know who I am?" he yelled after her, despite the fact that she was already gone.

Theory looked at the wig in his hand almost obsessively. He couldn't not look. Confusion washed over his face, and finally he stumbled back to the sofa where he collapsed in an emotional mess, clutching the wig as if it were the last remnant of a rope that kept him sane.

"I miss you," he cried.

The poor soul stared at the empty wig as if seriously expecting it to be refilled with the spirit of his lost soulmate. He cried in the pain one might equivocate with the longing for something precious that was never to be returned.

CHAPTER 13

Selena sat in the research lab comparing photos of the crime scene and those she had discovered from one hundred years prior. It seemed clear that whatever had happened in one period of time had happened in the other. In both scenes the skin was draped as if it were a coat that had been removed and flung over a chair almost errantly—but it wasn't a coat, it was human flesh, devoid apparently of anything that once resided within its confines.

The door to the lab opened. Selena turned to see Harris Barnes, the senior and most trusted lab rat. She stared at him, asking with her eyes for answers. Harris stood there, wanting to give her everything—he had a crush on Selena, as most the men and some of the women at the Center did.

Harris was forty-six years old, a self-professed science geek, who had been toying around with lab kits since he had been a young boy. He was recruited into the Black Syndicate in his younger years when it was clear that he had exceptional aptitude in the lab. It was a high school professor that began his successful wooing, easily winning the young Harris over by lauding his passionate pursuits in science, as opposed to his fellow students who chided him for the very same endeavor. He was seduced by the dark side easily enough, and now he was their head scientist. Maybe his crush on Selena was due to the fact the poor guy had no social life, or maybe it was just that science dorks always think that beauty will fall for the geek.

"What have you got?" she asked, breaking the strange silence.

"Nothing—literally, there is nothing. No soft tissue, no bone; there is just skin."

"That's it?"

"The only other thing I could find was necrotic tissue."

"Well, isn't that par for the course, with a dead skin?"

"Sure, under normal circumstances, except aside from the tissue being necrotic, I can't identify the origin of the sample."

"What do you mean the origin?"

"There exists a second sample that didn't originate in the host. The tissue is necrotic, as I said, but it has a DNA signature I am not familiar with."

"Harris, let me see if I have this right. You found dead tissue of some unknown origin within the remains of the what was left of our dead comrade?"

Harris nodded. "Pretty much."

"Any theories?"

"Whatever killed him may have been parasitic in nature. I think whatever did this to Samuel Black, literally did it from the inside out. The tissue left behind may have been some sort of waste from the consumption of the victim's insides."

"If that is true, what happened to the parasite?"

"The only logical conclusion I can come to is that whatever did this entered the body and then exited."

"So, if that were the case, wouldn't there be some sort of other evidence in the victim's home of whatever did this?"

"You would think. We are scouring the evidence and the home."

"A parasite that eats everything in a human but the skin?"

"That's what I am guessing. The good news is that it seems to be rare, if the only two cases are 100 years apart."

"That, and whoever is doing the eating has a taste for our kind."

"What do you mean?" Harris asked

"The other known victim was a Black operative."

"Shit, that is odd."

"That it is, Harris; that it is. Let me know if they find anything at the crime scene."

Harris nodded and his eyes drank in Selena one last time before exiting, hoping that he didn't give away his longing for her as much as he did.

CHAPTER 14

The two men lay in the soft cloud bed that cost more than it was worth. Simeon, unlike his new lover, spent all his hard-earned money on luxuries. The entire flat was immaculate, as if there were constant people in to clean, buff, and shine every nook and cranny. The place had a glean that reflected the fastidiousness of its occupant.

Simeon dressed to impress but he also lived to impress. Perhaps he was simply overcompensating for growing up with nothing, always trying to prove to himself and the rest of the world that he had made it, despite being raised from the dirt of Louisiana. He had left all that behind, and unlike his new lover, he felt the need to tell himself and the rest of the world he had arrived and was here to stay.

Eli, on the other hand, was experiencing a bunch of firsts. First-time sex with Simeon, first time at his apartment, first time enjoying the pleasure of sin and excess—how had he not enjoyed this before? His phone rang.

"Do you have to get that?" Simeon asked.

Eli looked at his phone and grimaced. "Yeah, I should. Hello?" he answered.

Eli got out of the cloud bed and paced as he nodded and mixed in an "uh-huh" and "I see" in between steps.

Simeon watched Eli pace, his cock swinging in rhythm with his steps like an elephant swinging its trunk. Simeon admired his new lover's entire body. It was lean and sinewy, and the cuts of where all his muscles were so pronounced.

"I am very sorry. Of course, we will take care of it. Thank you for alerting me." Eli ended the call.

"Problem?"

"Fucking Theory; he is scaring the women. He gets too fucked up, but how can I stop him? The escort service brings him more drugs and he is drinking more and more."

"He will calm down," Simeon suggested.

"I don't think so. He is getting worse," Eli said, getting dressed.

Simeon stood up and grabbed Eli, kissing him passionately. "Maybe we should let him go down whatever dark road he needs to travel."

"You're kidding, right? You want us both to be out of a job? The way you live, I doubt you can afford it."

"We will take over. Co-host. The network is upset with him for not producing any new shows, but he is still operating a budget as if he is. His 'get out of jail free' card won't last forever."

"I dunno, Simeon."

Simeon nodded. "Theory is done. He is acting like a lunatic. He will get us all burned if we don't act."

"Yeah, but in the meantime, I need to go over there and sober him up."

"What you should do is push him further over the precipice."

"He doesn't seem to need help with that."

"Regardless, maybe leaving him some more party supplies will at least distract him while we do what we need to do. You saw who came looking for him last night, right? You think the Black Syndicate fucks around?"

Simeon went into a drawer and produced two vials of white powder. He brought them to Eli, who stared at the powder-filled containers.

"Keeping him high serves us how? He's a mess enough as it is. It could backfire, and we lose the show along with him."

Simeon threw his arms around Eli. "You worry too much. I am sure you are aware of my capabilities. Trust me when I tell you I know what I am doing."

Eli was smitten with Simeon—the attention, sexually, affection, and just the fact that he seemed to want to be friends and work together. Even though he was a good assistant to Theory, he never believed Simeon respected or even liked him, let alone this. It was validation that he sopped up like a hungry sponge. He took the vials.

"This is what he wants, Eli. He is done. All Theory is focused on is trying to fill the void left by her—it's pathetic. He isn't going to come back from it. It's our time now."

Eli nodded as he put the vials in his pocket. "I had a good time. It was my first time with a man."

"I wouldn't have known. Maybe we just have great chemistry."

Eli felt awash with wantedness. His cock grew again in his pants, full of desire. He didn't want to leave, but he knew he had to go, for more than one reason. "I should go."

Eli kissed Simeon again, thinking that this never would happen again. He tried to savor the moment while it lasted.

CHAPTER 15

Selena was looking at surveillance video of the building where people had a habit of falling to their deaths. She had the dates of the three people who had died there—two women and one man had lost their lives there in the last few months.

It was just as Simeon White had said; the production crew came out of the building and scattered like cockroaches after the lights had been turned on. The first time they had eluded authorities—the second time they weren't so lucky, but they were cleared of any wrongdoing. They had video footage of the woman leaping off the roof of the building. It was supposed to be a dramatization for the show, and it ended in tragedy.

Simeon told Selena that Theory was in an adjacent building, and she had footage of him in an elevator, coming and going from said building, but what good did that do her? All of this proved nothing, but perhaps they didn't know that. Guilty consciences were prone to plenty of doubt. It would be a well-planted seed, and Selena was an experienced gardener.

"What am I missing?" she asked herself.

She paced while she wondered. Finally, she exited the room and went straight to Major Ott's office. To gain access to her superior, she had to negotiate several security layers: hand scans, ocular scans, access codes, at every step. Sometimes it made her miss the days when there was just a human gatekeeper. Sterility was now the name in the security game; sterility was just the name of the world now. People who forgot to even speak to each other, dates that were consummated with a review or the swipe of a finger—why should a secret initiative be any different? It was all the same. No wonder investigative work had become so much more complicated. It lacked the human interaction that the world was slowly losing—or was it already lost?

Selena reached Ott's office and was left with one scan to go if the major was in. Under normal circumstances she would have arranged the meeting, but her compulsion carried her there without forewarning.

The door opened for her without a scan or input of any kind. The burly man she had known all her life sat as if he knew she was coming. Perhaps he had watched her via the cameras in the hallway and deduced her intent.

"You must have had one helluva idea. I can't remember the last time I got an unannounced visit."

"Sorry, Major. It's this Theory business."

"You have a real hard-on for this asshole—why? It's not really our purview."

"I know, sir. As to why, I cannot say. It's something I cannot explain."

"I appreciate your candor, Selena. What do you want?"

"Approval for surveillance 24/7."

"What has this civilian done?"

"It appears that he may be murdering people, using his show as a cover."

"So, you are saying this is a conspiracy, from a conspiracy theorist?"

"I never thought of it like that, sir, but I am not sure what this is. All I can tell you is that I am drawn to whatever is going on, as if I have a connection to it in some odd way."

Ott considered for a moment. "Only because it's you and this guy is a grade-A asshole, I will give you a week. If you need more after that, we will have to meet again."

"Thank you, sir."

Selena turned to leave.

"Selena, make sure this is by the book. It makes me nervous that you somehow are taking this personally with this guy."

Selena looked at her superior. He was correct, although she didn't know why. It was just that spooky feeling that she needed to do this. Instinct was always a better guide to the truth than reason, and Selena always trusted her instincts.

CHAPTER 16

Theory sat in his usual stupor—perhaps worse; vodka bottles were strewn about him on the sofa, almost lying there with him in the same empty state. The depression had set in hard, it always did when the sun came up and he was out of drugs and booze and the numbness was wearing off and the self- hatred was settling back in, hangover in tow.

The sun was rising outside, but setting inside Theory's world. Every time he failed at getting answers, he invited death; the more the failures that added up, the stronger the pull felt from the darkness. There was an answer; he could feel it in what was left of his bones that he hadn't destroyed with his overindulgence. Something in the universe told him she was somewhere, alive, and he didn't know which ate at his soul more: the fact that she was out there somewhere or the fact that he couldn't figure out what happened and how to get her back.

"You worry too much, love," she said.

The voice was an elixir to his pain. On some level he knew that she was just in his mind, but the need to believe she was actually there was greater.

The woman's arms wrapped around the broken man. It was his only comfort, even if it was in his imagination. How pathetic had he become—his loss consumed him, like a cosmic stop sign telling him for whatever reason that his life just had no meaning without her. Theory knew that she wasn't dead; if she were, there would have been a body on the cement under the building like the others he sent flying off it. No, she was not dead, but she was very gone and it ate his soul from the inside out. These visits were all that kept Theory tethered to sanity.

"I am lost without you," he said, his voice thick with desperation.

She sighed.

"Please, let me see you," he begged.

"It's not possible, my love. You have to trust me."

"I need to see you again," he insisted.

"You will—just not how you think."

"Is it true?" he asked as his eyes became moist.

"I would never lie to you, Elysium, but I have to go. You have a visitor coming."

She squeezed him, or he imagined that she did, but then her arms slipped away as if they were never there. Of course, that was because they never were.

A knock came at the door. Theory didn't answer. Keys jingled after another unsuccessful knock, and the door opened. Theory didn't move. He knew it was Eli; no one else had keys. He wanted to tell him to go away, but he couldn't muster the words in a meaningful way. Truth was, Eli was the only one who seemed to give a shit, so despite the impulse to push him away, he didn't do it. Eli appeared before him wearing a look of concern— or was it disdain? Theory couldn't handle being judged, especially since the drugs and alcohol were wearing off.

"Did I miss a meeting or something?" Theory asked weakly.

"I came to check on you, Theory. Besides, you haven't produced a new show in almost two months."

Theory nodded.

"There are other issues at hand," Eli continued.

Theory looked at him like a punished child.

"The service you use is having reservations about sending the women; you are scaring them. I think they expect a number of the clients to be fucked up on whatever, but if you give the impression you might hurt them, they won't give a shit who you are or who you used to be. You know who runs those services? I will tell you. Criminals—bad ones. They know who you are, and obviously with the amount of business you give them, finding you isn't an issue."

Theory nodded.

"They aren't the only ones who have reason to come after you. We had a visit from the Black Syndicate at the office after your last experiment.

Man, have you given them about a billion reasons to come after you and the rest of us! I can't believe they didn't shut us down right then and there and take you away for good. Perhaps it was just a warning."

Theory didn't think he could break down much further. He was broken into so many pieces already that he was able to keep it together only with numbness, the elixir of all that kills us from the inside.

"I need...."

"Some of this?" Eli asked, producing the vials that Simeon had given him.

Theory leapt up from the sofa and grabbed the container from Eli. He deftly spread out the powder on the coffee table and took a healthy snort. He closed his eyes as he bathed in the drug's embrace.

"Maybe you should stay in for a few days, while things get sorted with the Black Syndicate," Eli suggested, placing the other vial on the table next to the Tony Montana pile Theory had made from the first container.

"Yes, yes—laying low is the plan. You are a good man, Eli," Theory said at a hundred miles an hour.

"I think it's a good idea if we get the show back on its feet, too. We are ready to produce new segments. The network can't take much more hiatus."

"Who is *we*?" Theory asked.

"Simeon and I can do it until you are ready to come back."

"You and Simeon? Working together?"

"Yeah, we have to, for the sake of the show."

"Whatever. I'll believe it when I see it. But before you and that asshole make nice, order me a case of vodka, and call the service. I don't want to be alone while I lay low.'"

"Of course. I will get right on it."

Eli stood there for a moment, as if he believed that Theory would realize that there was a coup in place and get his shit together, but all the man seemed to care about was feeding his vices and forgetting all that he had lost. Finally, Eli turned and left, leaving behind any respect he had left for his mentor.

CHAPTER 17

Simeon sat at Theory's desk. He should not have been there, but he was. It was premature, but Simeon had gone beyond caring; he was thirsty to take what he felt he was entitled to. He would be the new Elysium Theory. He was responsible for increasing his popularity with the wisp of white hair concept that caught fire and more than doubled his fan base.

Simeon had something to prove. His father had told him he would fail at everything he would ever do, and that he would never amount to anything. That kind of abuse of a child doesn't go without consequences. Simeon knew his father was just an angry drunk, and his father's father had probably unleashed the same rage on him. Generations of abuse was a cycle that Simeon planned on ending, and his particular end was to succeed beyond even his wildest imagination, and in the process hopefully give that prick of a father something to watch. Every night Simeon would be on, that asshole would eat his words and his abusive actions.

Simeon looked about the office. There were framed promotional posters festooning the walls, and a golden microphone sat in front of Simeon on the desk along with a single photograph of *her*. It was uncanny how similar they looked; almost identical. He studied the image. The woman in the photo had the wisp of white in her hair, while her doppelgänger did not.

"Trying it on?"

Simeon looked up to see Eli leaning in the doorway. This was a first, the two of them buddy/buddy in the office was off-putting, but Simeon brought this on himself. Much to his chagrin, he was actually liking Eli more than he wanted to.

"It's not the first time," Simeon admitted. "Have you?"

"Of course I have."

There was a hint of uncertainty between the men. They had worked in the same space for years, but now there was an actual sense of working together for the first time, and neither knew quite what to do.

"Did you see him?" Simeon asked.

"He is all over the place but was also happy to stay numb. I just hope it doesn't kill him. The escorts are getting more nervous around him; some of the services are hesitant to even send anyone."

"As long as he is distracted."

"I dunno what the women bring from the service, but I'm fairly sure it is about half of what you gave me to give him. Plus, I ordered a case of booze, and more women. I assume they will have more drugs with them."

"You didn't make sure of it?" Simeon asked, a little disappointed.

"I don't want to kill him, Simeon."

"He's doing it to himself, Eli."

"We are enabling him, so we can take the show. We have some responsibility, don't we?"

Simeon shrugged. "I'm not sure if we can be responsible for his downfall. Theory has been fucking himself."

"I guess what is done is done. I just don't feel good about it."

"Neither do I," Simeon lied.

"Maybe we can get him into a rehab? That would give us time to get the show up and running again, and we would be helping him," Eli suggested.

"Theory doesn't want help. He has lost her, he has lost his show; his identity has been reduced to perpetual numbness and anger. That's who he is now. We can't do shit about it except honor what he built here. As they say, 'The show must go on.'"

Eli nodded. He was stuck in an odd position. He wanted to please Simeon, he wanted to save Theory, but he had no idea how to manage himself. It was his own damage, trying to please everyone. He wondered if Simeon knew this about him, if he was just a pawn, or maybe he was just being insecure. This was a lousy lot to have in life, and he knew it.

"You're right, it does. The show is what matters." Eli paused. "I want to show you something."

"OK."

Simeon watched with curiosity as Eli opened up the file on Theory's computer. He played the cryptic, static-laden message.

"It sounds like he is saying a war is coming. We need to clean it up—the feed is fucked—but there is something familiar about it."

Eli nodded. "What does it mean? And I tried to trace it, nothing. No IP address; it's like it dropped in out of nowhere."

"It does seem like there is something to this. Let's get some of the tech guys to see if they can clean it up for us. Whatever this is, it can be your piece—you found it, you report on it."

Eli smiled. The idea turned him on. Maybe if they succeeded, he would finally move out of the shithole he had told himself he deserved.

"What kind of production budget do we have?"

"Ha! Now you are talking! Don't worry about that; the tech guys are on salary. Find out what it is and what it means, and we will go from there."

Eli paused. He didn't know if he should look at Simeon as a producer or as his lover. He wanted the latter, but he didn't have the confidence to kiss him or ask if they could fuck again in his apartment, or maybe even share a meal. So he turned and left.

"I enjoyed the time we spent together. Maybe we can hang out again?" Simeon said, expertly sensing the room.

Eli turned and nodded. "I would like that."

CHAPTER 18

Selena wondered if it was a mistake. She knew that she was breaking protocol, but something told her that she should. Selena was usually more pragmatic than to listen to instinct, but she couldn't help herself. She had brought some men with her as a precaution. She was sure that Theory had become homicidal, despite the fact that she was having issues proving it. Yet somehow, for some reason, she was drawn to confront him.

Selena left the men outside the building. Oddly, when she entered the building the door man smiled at her, and said, "Go right up, I'm sure he is expecting you."

Selena kept going as if this were perfectly normal, when in fact it was not. She was willing to flash her credentials, but this was better—there would be no warning.

Selena got in the elevator and turned and looked at the doorman, half expecting him to change his mind, but he wasn't even looking her way. The man was looking at a tablet of some kind. *This is too easy.*

Selena depressed the button to the eleventh floor. She started to get a bit nervous; something was off. Maybe it was her own behavior. This was just uncharacteristic of her and went against every Black Syndicate protocol. Selena was operating without a safety net. The sound of the bell when she passed each floor seemed to be ringing from inside her head. Finally, she got to the eleventh floor. She got out and looked around and instinctively turned and headed down to the right. Although she had never been to this building or Theory's flat specifically, it was if she had been. She came to the apartment door, Theory's door, number 1111, only to see that it was already ajar. Selena stared at the door. She turned to leave. She turned back. She turned to leave again.

"Hey!" His voice creaked.

Selena turned to see her target. Discomfort flooded her body. She knew she had miscalculated, but she stood firm.

Theory looked like Hell's hurricane had hammered him. The man looked frail and disheveled, and if she hadn't been in a luxury apartment staring at a celebrity, she could easily have believed that she was in some seedy area of town face to face with a homeless, desperate man.

Theory squinted at Selena. She stood silently, paralyzed by his eyes boring into her soul.

"It's you. It's really you?"

"Mr. Theory, I am Selena Black. I shouldn't really be here, but...."

Theory moved to Selena and embraced her. He held on so tight she thought he might suffocate her with the strength of his grip. There was such desperation embedded in the affection.

"Mr. Theory, please..." Selena said, successfully breaking the embrace.

Theory drank her in again. "You are the best one they have ever sent to me. I mean you are exactly what I wanted. Exactly. Come inside; let's get started."

This guy is clearly gone. Selena stood there while Theory took her hand and led her inside. His touch was delicate and caring. She had really gotten herself into something that she shouldn't have, that much was clear, but she was in it, so Selena decided that she should make the most of it and went with him inside.

Selena took in the apartment. It was large and beautiful, but it looked as if a tornado had whipped through it. There was a pile of white powder sitting on the glass coffee table, some of it sifted into neat white lines. Keeping the lines and pile company was a liter of vodka in a fancy bottle. Theory caught Selena staring at his wares of mind-numbing addiction.

"Would you like some?" Theory offered leading his guest to the table.

"No, I am here...."

"Ha! That's just so authentic—the real Selena wouldn't have imbibed either! Which agency are you from? We must tell Eli. He has really found the best one this time. So many of the others were just not right."

"Mr. Theory, I believe you are mistaking me for someone else, I am Selena Black. I work for the syndicate. You have mentioned us often on your show."

Theory looked at Selena curiously. He sat down and snorted some of the white powder and poured himself a shot, which he downed right away. His mind was filled with questions. "This is a new twist, and I like it."

Selena looked at him incredulously. "No, there is no twist."

"Drink?" he offered.

"No, as I mentioned, I am here in an official capacity."

"That's right, you are," Theory smiled, and began to unbuckle his pants.

Selena stood suddenly as she realized what the man expected to happen. "This was a mistake, coming here."

"Coming here is what you were paid to do, bitch," Theory told her as he struggled with his belt.

"It seems both of us have miscalculated," Selena said.

She moved to the door when something strange happened. There was wind, indoors—it was beyond disconcerting, even under the obvious circumstances.

Theory stood, his belt hanging like a flaccid dog's tail, but his pants remained upright somehow.

Selena knew that Theory was seriously incapacitated, but she was also in a surveillance subject's home unofficially—it was bad, bad, bad. She flung open the door, and seemingly the unnatural wind produced a stronger gust. There was a zip of red lightning in the corridor. Selena, who didn't scare easily, was feeling uneasy. Part of it was her own doing for putting herself in the subject's domicile to begin with, but there was an indoor storm brewing that freaked her out even more than the misguided man she had come to visit.

Selena fought against the unnatural wind and made it into the hallway. It was as if she were stuck in some odd vacuum cleaner. She could see more red lightning at the end of the corridor too, but it also zipped behind her. Panic began to overtake her. It got worse when she saw powder-blue hands come out of seemingly thin air.

Selena was briefly paralyzed but snapped out of her fear and ran. There was one problem: there was lightning and wind coming from the end of the corridor she was running toward as well. She stopped as she saw that whatever was happening on one end of the corridor, was also happening on the other. A pair of powder-blue hands with symbols on them were tearing the fabric of space and time and coming into the hallway.

Selena felt a tug at her hand and was pulled out of her paralysis. Despite her initial fear that the hand that had grabbed her was of the supernatural variety, it was not. Theory, despite his inebriated state, had managed to see the danger Selena was in and come to the rescue.

"Come on, we need to get out of here!"

Selena didn't question him, just allowed herself to be led back into his apartment. He closed and locked the door behind them.

"Theory, I think we need to get out of the building!"

"That's what we are doing!"

Selena questioned his sanity, but after what she had just seen, she also questioned her own. She looked through the peep hole and saw that the two almost identical creatures where moving toward each other in the hallway. One had an Omega symbol on his back. Both creatures were nude, covered in tattoos of archaic symbols. Selena watched through the hole as the twin creatures grappled with each other.

"We need to get out of here NOW—come on!" Theory said to her.

Selena turned to him. All she saw was the balcony. *He wants to jump.* "What exactly did you have in mind?"

"Do you trust me?"

"No, Theory, I don't."

"Fine, you want to stay in here and see if those things are going to come in and get you? They seemed fascinated by you, not me, but you know what? I'm not going to guess at that. I'm going to get the fuck out of here."

Selena knew he was right, they needed to get out, but then again, this man was a drug-addled lunatic. Theory left the room. Selena weighed her options and looked through the eye hole again. The creatures were grappling, and from the sounds of it, forcefully throwing each other against the wall. While they looked almost identical, they were not. The one had an Omega symbol on his back, but the other had an "A" on his back instead.

What seemed clear was that if they stopped destroying Theory's hallway, they could come in the flat and come for them. The Omega throttled the Alpha, stunning his twin. He turned, seemingly looking at Selena despite the fact she was behind a door and completely out of sight.

"Shit!" Selena said, scared, as she saw the Omega walk toward her.

Selena turned to see where Theory was. She couldn't see him, but she heard him in another room.

"Theory!"

"In here!"

She was going to him, but it was too late. The door broke down and the muscular, powder-blue tattooed man came through what was left of the doorway.

Selena and the creature stood staring at each other. There was a moment of stillness that seemed to last longer than the second it was.

"Hey!" Theory yelled.

Both the creature and Selena were momentarily distracted by Theory. He was wielding a broomstick.

"I'm not sure pissing this thing off is such a good idea," Selena suggested.

Theory didn't deviate his gaze from the creature. Selena looked back to it, and it back to her. He squinted at her, obviously it decided that Theory and his broomstick were not a credible threat. It began to walk to toward Selena who, in turn, backed up slowly.

"If this thing kills me and you somehow survive, there are Black Syndicate men waiting for me outside. You tell them what happened."

"Nothing is going to happen," Theory said. "The closet in the bedroom has a secret exit."

The man moved on the creature and swung the broomstick. It shattered upon contacting the creature, but it didn't seem to even register it. It just kept advancing on Selena. She managed to get by the creature and to the closet in the bedroom. There was a hole in the wall, and she knew it was down the rabbit hole or down for good. The Omega was closing on her, and …down the rabbit hole she went. The Omega went into the same unknown.

Theory rushed to the room. He saw the two disappear into nothingness, leaving only a zip of red lightning in their wake. Theory collapsed. He was facing the door where the second creature had recovered and advanced on Theory. He was too tired to fight, but the creature wasn't looking for one.

The creature looked at the lump of a man that Theory was, leaning against the balcony. Then the creature turned away and jumped into a mirror as if it were a swimming pool. The glass appeared to liquefy enough for the Alpha to disappear into the glass before it solidified again, as if he had never been there.

The men that had accompanied Selena entered Theory's apartment. They could see that there had been a torrent of activity. They came in like a surgical strike team, clearing the empty spaces one by one. Finally, when they saw that there was no threat, they approached the one person left from the ordeal.

"Where is she?"

Theory was slumped and weeping, like the broken soul that he had become.

"WHERE THE FUCK IS SHE?"

One of the men picked up Theory by his loose-fitting shirt. It was violent, but the odd thing was that Theory didn't protest or fight back; he just hung there like an old bathrobe that has sat unused on the same hook for years.

The man who held Theory was obviously upset, but one of his coworkers calmed him by placing a hand on his arm.

"He obviously doesn't know," the man told his angered companion.

The man holding Theory lowered him. "Cuff him; he's coming with us."

The third man in black did as was asked. Theory was cuffed, a shroud tossed over his head, and he was led away to a place where most people were never seen nor heard from ever again.

PART TWO

CHAPTER 1

Captain Wu sat ramrod straight at his desk. In fact, everything in the small office was regimented. Photographs on the wall were lined up in perfect symmetry. They were all of people in military uniforms, including a child who resembled Wu.

Everything was grey—not just in the photos, but seemingly in the room and outside the window in the courtyard as well. This place had the ambience of the most boring place in the world, but in truth it was far from boring.

There was a knock at the door. It was a stern, yet respectful knock. Wu looked up from whatever had his attention on his desk and uttered the word that made the person on the other end feel safe enough to enter.

The man who entered was an adjunct. He was also in a grey uniform and saluted rigidly as soon as he positioned himself in front of Wu's desk.

"Speak," Wu instructed the man.

"She is back."

Wu stared at the man, almost in disbelief. Then he stood, almost perfectly, his posture unwavering as he clasped his hands behind his back and maneuvered around the adjunct.

"This is unexpected," Wu said.

The adjunct nodded in agreement.

"I assume she has been brought to the tombs for debrief?" Wu asked.

"Yes, sir, she is being transported to medical to make certain she was stable and while I informed you, of course."

Wu looked at the man, proud in a way, because he had done everything as he should have. Wu was really pleased with himself. This was his doing, training the men in such a way that everything ran spot on. Wu moved to the door, and as if in perfect synchronicity the adjunct moved ahead of him and opened the door, and he followed his commander out of the office and into the bowels of the compound.

Outside it was as grey as it was inside, as if the place had a permanent overcast spell placed upon it. Wu walked stiffly, and with purpose as his adjunct followed loyally, almost mirroring his posture and gait. Even the ground seemed grey, as the sound of Wu's military boots crunched on the gravel.

Wu didn't look at any of the activity around him, yet there was plenty going on. Men and women in simple grey cloth, torn shirts, and matching ragged pants were chained in groups adhering to various tasks. Some of the people in the chain gang looked familiar, almost the spitting images of the crew that were on the roof of the skyscraper when the young man jumped to his death.

The people in captivity cowered as Wu passed them, despite the fact that he paid them no mind. Some of them hit the deck in fear, balled up, and shivered until one uniformed guard with a whip cracked the scared prisoners back into work.

The courtyard was a portrait of human misery. It wasn't just the obvious pain of the prisoners; the captors too seemed weighed down by a heavy sadness that could never be recovered from. Happiness died here long, long ago, and it seemed clear it would never live in any of these souls again. Pain and suffering were the emotions du jour, all day, every day.

Wu walked past all of it, as if none of it and none of them were even there.

Wu was treated with respect, whether from the prisoners who feared him or the guards who aspired to be like him. There couldn't have been a deeper dichotomy, but whether this man garnered fear or adoration, Wu was clearly one of those immovable forces in the universe, and he knew it.

Wu stopped in his tracks and the adjunct, who followed so diligently behind, came within a hair's breadth of running right into his superior. A bead of anxiety-filled sweat appeared on his brow as Wu turned to address him.

"Where?"

"Sir?"

"When she returned, where was it she materialized?" Wu asked.

"One of the dormitories."

Wu considered this. "Strange, isn't it? Of course, I had hoped we could get her back, but I wasn't sure it was possible."

The adjunct stood expectantly. He assumed Wu would say something else, or direct an order, but he did not. Instead, he turned and walked off toward the tombs, and his man followed loyally behind him.

CHAPTER 2

The tombs were aptly named. The caves were nestled deep into one side of the mountains that surrounded the 5-Gen. "5-Gen" was the name of the prison, and it was also aptly named. 5-Gen stood for 5 generations, meaning that 5 generations of some families were kept in this hellhole. Escape, for all intents and purposes, was impossible.

The impossible had happened, in a matter of speaking. She had returned, when Wu didn't even know that she could, that the bridge between worlds was a two-way route. Even as Wu walked to debrief her, he questioned if what he was about to see was even possible.

Selena was in a room used for interrogations. It made her nervous, since she wasn't a prisoner and was unlikely to be interrogated. She was a willing participant in Wu's plan. She figured that this was a good place where secrets could be properly kept, and Selena was right. There was one problem: she hadn't planned on falling in love. It wasn't part of the mission parameters. It was a side effect of the seduction.

Selena missed him. She touched the wisp of white that was in her otherwise raven hair. She pulled it down, the white wisp, in a pathetic display of sentimentality. She wasn't supposed to fall, she was supposed to pretend to fall, but the Theory from the other side wasn't like the one from this side. Sure, they must share some common tones, but to her, he couldn't be more different. She had fallen in love with the doppelgänger of the man she had been conditioned to hate.

The Theory responsible for so much chaos in the 5-Gen, and the Theory *over there* simply weren't the same man. Sure, similar, but the two men were very different. Yet despite the differences, there was much to be learned from the version of the man from the other universe.

Selena looked around the room. She sat at a grey table, metallic, but worn badly, with scrapes and gouges. There was even dried blood from Lord knows what they were torturing out of someone.

The room itself was carved out of a cave, the moisture and humidity heavy. In some parts of the room, there were drips running down some of the uneven walls, and as Selena looked at them she wondered why she was there. It was part existential question, but also part local one. She was an agent of Wu's back from a mission that no one knew she would ever return from. It could have been a one-way trip, or when she jumped from the building, she had no way of knowing if the height of the skyscraper would provide the location and velocity to the 5-Gen she had hoped that would enable her to get back. Selena was becoming angry that she seemed to be treated like a prisoner, but perhaps that wasn't what this was.

The 5-Gen population was comprised of prisoners and keepers. There was no middle ground, so the place wasn't designed for a debriefing although it was, in essence, a military grade compound. Perhaps, Selena thought, this was the best place for a debriefing. But what if Wu didn't trust her anymore? The tombs, beyond being used for interrogation, were also used for segregation

Selena had seen what it was like to be in the worst accommodations in the 5-Gen. She herself had spent her life there, as her family worked for Wu's father, just like she worked for Wu. Generations of prisoners were confined for life; but the guards were lifers too.

Selena was filled with uncertainty. Perhaps it was a residual effect of the travel between worlds, or the stress of leaping off a building to take such a journey. Still, she had enjoyed a freedom in the other world that had been a foreign, yet welcome respite from 5-Gen life. But she had done her job, to a degree, and returned, which was double icing on the cake, since the road between worlds wasn't exactly a well-traveled one.

Selena had known Wu to be a ruthless commander, just like his father and grandfather before him. It was the waiting that made her imagination kick into high gear. It's always the worst in life when we are alone with our thoughts to make us feel smaller and more frightened than need be. Still, it was the way of the human mind.

Selena thought about standing up to pace but talked herself out of it. She didn't want to appear nervous and give Wu pause. He would want to see her right away, she thought—or did he want to prime her by having her sit and wonder what he would do to her?

Fortunately, Selena didn't have long to wait. The door shot open with authority and Wu came in, his trusted adjunct holding the door. Wu waved him off, and the door shut behind him as he left.

Selena stood and gave Captain Wu the customary salute, hoping that his intent would be clear off the bat, but it was not. Wu seemed always to have only one look: stern.

She stood ramrod straight as Wu simply stared at her. He was known for making people feel discomfort, but she had managed to circumvent that for the most part, until now. Wu circled Selena, assessing every nook and cranny of his officer, looking for differences—or was it for betrayal? Finally, he stopped in front of her.

"Sit," Wu instructed.

Selena sat in the metallic chair that wobbled unevenly as she settled into it. Wu placed his hands on the table in front of her and stared in like a slithery serpent.

"What is this?" Wu said, flicking at the wisp of white in her otherwise black hair.

"Part of the cover, for the other Theory, sir. Over there he is a celebrity of sorts. This is a show of support to his cause over there."

"So, he is a troublemaker in both worlds?" Wu paused. "Did you run into my counterpart?"

"No sir."

"Did you run into yours?"

"No, but I admit I looked into her as best I could. Her life is not an open book; the normal research protocols in their world didn't allow me much."

Wu stared at Selena. "And what about the target?"

"Theory is as outspoken in that world as he is in ours."

"Yes, but what did you learn that could help us eliminate him from our side?"

"He has vulnerabilities, addictions. He can become enslaved to them."

"What are these vulnerabilities?"

"Alcohol, cocaine, perhaps anything that will give him a rush. He will chase any high to stave off his boredom. He is exceptionally intelligent, but what comes with that is a high level of understanding of the pain in the world, and he suffers. He is desperate not to feel those things."

"What about you? Did you make yourself an addict, too?"

Selena looked at Wu in the hopes that her feelings for Theory in the other world wouldn't betray her. "I just did what needed doing, for the sake of our survival."

Wu considered her. "So, the Theory from our world could be suscep-tible to your affections? We could use that?"

"He is vulnerable to a number of proclivities, but as far as I can tell, even though they are most definitely similar, they are not exact. The Theory that eludes you here, who wishes to overthrow you, may not suc-cumb to the same vulnerabilities."

Anger washed over Wu's face, and he slammed his hand down on the table, causing it to jump up. It startled Selena, too.

"Eludes me?!"

"Captain, sir, I mean no disrespect. I went to great lengths, at excep-tional risk to my own life, to go to the other side for you and for the benefit of our world. Surely, you must understand how dedicated I am to finding the rebel and taking him down. When I say eludes you, I mean the embodiment of our world, which undoubtedly you are the unquestioned substance and stability of."

Wu softened. This was a man who never softened, but Selena managed to elicit it anyway. She was his most trusted underling—a woman, no less, but she was who she was to him, regardless of gender. His father, who ran the 5-Gen before Wu did, trusted Selena's father as much as Wu trusted

Selena. Of course, Wu consulted both men before making the move, but more out of respect, than due to a lack of self-confidence.

"Theory from our side *does* elude me," Wu admitted.

Selena nodded. "We will find him, Captain."

Wu had a rare look of compassion. "You are the only one who can know how much this pains me. My father and my grandfather before him never would have had this happen on their watch."

"Times are different, Captain. You shouldn't judge yourself based on the generations that came before you."

"How do you think they would have felt, knowing that their son and grandson allowed the impossible to happen?"

"You don't know that he has escaped," Selena rationalized.

"I do know, because he isn't here."

"There is only one place he could have gone, Selena."

"You think he figured out how to cross over?"

"I can't imagine what else is possible."

"You want me to go back, don't you?"

Wu nodded ever so slightly. "The possibility exists that what happens to your counterpart affects you."

"What is the mission, exactly, sir?"

"Kill Theory."

CHAPTER 3

Selena went back to the barracks. She was on orders to rest before she was to be examined again by Wu's medical and science team. Despite the grey, dank, spartan appearance of the 5-Gen, they invested heavily in science and tech. Wu's obsession with the other side had been carried over from his father, who also invested heavily in research.

She knew that the examination was to determine whether she was suitable to again make the journey between worlds. It was no easy task. It didn't matter; they would send her anyway. But if nothing else, they would study her, see if they could detect any after effects of the unorthodox travel, because undoubtedly, they would want to do it again and again until they could stop the adverse effects of whatever the spooky connection was.

Wu was convinced that the existence of the other world crushed their own—almost a cosmic Yin and Yang, a balance between worlds. As one prospered, the other became a living hell. This operating theory had been in the Wu family for three generations, which was when the existence of the parallel world was first discovered.

Selena didn't know what to believe, being the only person to live in both. Prior to her life in the other world, surely she did believe that the existence of the other world suffocated her own, but that was generationally conditioned, passed down again and again until repetition had morphed into truth. But that truth was in question. Things changed for Selena, and she made the mistake of falling for Theory. She couldn't help it. Love isn't so much a choice as it is an infectious virus of some sort, slowly spreading itself over one's soul until there is nothing left but that pure, oft-times pathetic yearning.

Selena sat on the cot. The mattress was uneven, and uncomfortable—that was life in the 5-Gen; everything caused some level of discomfort. Of course, the prisoners had the most miserable life one could imagine, but the guards were also sentenced to a shitty life, albeit better, but how much?

The cot was a sharp contrast to the days and nights spent in the luxury of *his* apartment. Selena closed her eyes and imagined herself next to Theory in the soft Egyptian cotton sheets. The mattress felt like one was sleeping on a cloud, the fluffy pillows, and his taut, lean body intertwined with hers like a pretzel.

Wu would have her killed if she were found out for falling in love with her target, especially the other of the man who tormented Wu on this side of the universe. Selena no longer knew what to believe. There was a war afoot inside her soul as well as between the two worlds, even if one didn't know about the existence of the other.

Selena used to get angry at the stories of how the other world's pleasure was her own's heavy pain. The 5-Gen was an ocean of misery, the waters thick with suffering. It wasn't just horrible for the prisoners; the guards all had life sentences too. No one ever left, except Selena, and she had to risk her life to do it.

The Theory from this side was an enigma. He was waging a guerilla war on Wu and his men—from where, no one knew. The rumors were that he had been the first and only escapee from the prison, but that may have just been all talk to rise the prisoners up in some false hope, or simply to motivate them to rise up against their jailers. Selena always believed that he somehow just evaded them, perhaps having a network of hiding places within the 5-Gen. It made the most sense; if someone could truly leave this hell, why would they ever return?

Selena didn't know what had transpired since she had been gone all those months, but she imagined the situation wasn't improving. The 5-Gen Theory was like an insect that had crawled under Wu's skin; no matter how much he scratched, the pest still persisted.

It didn't matter, Selena rationalized. What mattered was that she was going back, to be with him. Selena would not be able to carry out her mission. It tore at her soul.

Even though the 5-Gen had been all she had known, meeting Theory, her Theory, was a game-changer. The connection between the two was nothing short of otherworldly; everything seemed to be in its proper place with him. Of course, she was rife with conflict. Selena had been sent to gather information, to learn anything she could for the purpose of corralling the 5-Gen Theory. The plan had been to romantically involve herself, but she got more than she bargained for, and then some. That mission hadn't come with a kill order.

Did Wu believe that killing the other Theory would make Wu's nemesis disappear? Selena found it hard to believe it worked like that. There were similarities between the pairs of people that existed in both worlds, and they did have a spooky connection, to be sure, but certainly one dying in one world wouldn't cause death of their other in an alternative universe.

It didn't matter. Love trumped all. Selena would go back, and stay back, and that would be that. This was Selena's happily ever after, even if she had to defy space and time to do it.

It wasn't without concern. Wu had known her since they were both children, and he could read strangers deftly. Would he detect her love for the other of his enemy? Or that she had no intent of killing her target or coming back? The last part probably had no bearing. Wu didn't care if she returned; in all likelihood, he didn't expect her to make it back one time, let alone twice. The travel between worlds wasn't exactly a well-worn path. It required a leap of faith that Selena had taken once for the sake of her world and would again for the sake of love. Truth was, Wu must have figured she could have a better life over there. The 5-Gen was a heap of grey dust, surrounded by mountains; no one ever left. She questioned why she had come back—generations of loyalty, she suspected, but she had to fall off a skyscraper to do it, and she didn't know if it would work again.

Loving, as it turned out, was a complicated mess. Selena had never loved before, and she hoped for her sake that she would never love again, provided that she made it back to her Theory. She longed for him and berated herself for taking Theory up to the top of the building to explain who she was; instead, she had returned to this hell. Perhaps it was generations of loyalty that coursed through her blood and bones. Selena couldn't decide if her coming back was an accident or subconsciously purposeful. She had meant to take Theory up there to come clean, but something happened. Perhaps it was the pull of the other universe that was so strong in that spot and yanked her back, as if to course-correct her being in a place that she never should have been at all. Selena decided that if she did get back to him, she wouldn't bother to try and explain where she disappeared to when she was sucked off that skyscraper, and that the important thing was that she was back, and she would stay, and they could never go near that building again. In fact, she was hoping that if she made it back, they could run away from that place, where no rift in space or time could suck her back to the hellhole that was the 5-Gen.

CHAPTER 4

Wu walked in the dusty, grey yard. He was at the height of his paranoia. His eyes shifted, looking for his dark-haired nemesis around every turn, yet he saw nothing.

He was under tremendous pressure. Running the 5-Gen had been his birthright, and he would one day pass the mantle on to his son, but not if he couldn't solve the insurrection from within. Theory from this world gave hope to the prisoners that they might not have to live like this, how it had been for generations. The prisoners couldn't be led to believe anything other than that this was as good as it would ever get. Assuming they would do their labor- intensive jobs in exchange for some shitty gruel and a place to sleep, they would keep on going as they had for generations before them.

Wu was losing his grip on his command, but also on himself. It was a slow descent into madness, triggered by a ghost of a man who seemed to torment Wu at every turn. Wu would see the dark-haired man, standing in a corner, or through a mirror, but upon further inspection, the man wasn't really there.

Wu needed to be in command, and to do that he needed to regain command of his senses. He walked to the factory, where the garments were made for both the keepers and the kept, although the kept did all the work. The population of the 5-Gen was subjugated; they were slaves who barely existed according to rules of being alive.

The factory was as gray as the rest of the prison, perhaps grayer, certainly more bleak. Wu felt great joy at the production and misery that the factory generated.

It was prime work hours, meaning that the path to the factory was clear, aside from the prisoners outside who swept the dust or moved boulders around. Guards with whips and batons laid into the beleaguered prisoners especially hard as Wu walked past. He smiled approvingly. Fear was the father of control.

Wu entered the concrete, windowless building with his trusty adjunct in tow and the glorious sounds of prisoners being whipped and beaten both behind and in front of him.

It was a massive open, grey space. The floor was filled with ten rows of ten workers, perfectly lined up at little tables. The tables had archaic sewing machines on them. On the perimeter of the floor, guards stood on platforms that surrounded the tables. On one side was a giant chalkboard, it was obviously a way to keep track of numbers of the product and productivity of each line.

The guards all stiffened even more than their rigid posture had previously allowed. The workers had their heads bowed in a slumped, submissive manner. Wu walked between some of the workers as if inspecting their stations, but truthfully, he was getting off on how scared they were of him.

Wu walked up to the board, staring up at the guards. "Are you pleased with the production numbers?" Wu asked.

"Yes, Captain, we maintain or exceed our numbers daily."

"Wonderful! Tell me, how are you managing to motivate this scum?"

The guard sniggered and rang the bell. A door opened and a prisoner scurried out. He carried a small tray. On the tray was a wooden spoon with a ball of rice on it. The prisoner stopped in front of the rows of laborers and held the tray perfectly still.

The guard rang the bell again, and the work began. The laborers sewed in a frenzy. It wasn't pretty; most of the workers were literally bleeding at the fingers as they worked with utter fury.

All ten workers, in all the ten rows, were making grey shirts. They were creating uniforms for themselves or other prisoners. When one worker finished a shirt, they lifted it up in the air, and a guard came and inspected it. If it was perfect, they took it to a bin; if it wasn't, they beat the worker briefly before throwing the garment on the floor, and the poor son of a bitch who made the mistake had to start again.

Finally, one row managed to finish ten shirts, and the guard waved to the platform where the bell-ringer chimed and everyone stopped. The bell rang again and the winning row stood. The bell rang again and the prisoner who held the tray with the spoon of rice approached the winning row. The tray- bearer stopped at every person, waiting until they took a minuscule portion of rice—but they didn't eat it, not just yet. They stared at it, waiting, almost savoring its minimalist nature.

Once everyone had a bit of what was on the spoon, the treat-bearer scuttled off back through the little portal from which he came, disappearing until the next contest, perhaps.

And then the bell rang again, and the winning line ate their pathetic, tiny reward, grateful for the small nutritional payment.

One of the sample garments was given to Wu, who looked at it, finally nodding to the guard who ran this shitty little operation. "Well done, very well done."

"Thank you, Captain."

Wu shuddered for a moment. He had a vision, an imagining, one of his terrors. Behind the guard he saw the black-haired Theory as he waved and smiled as if he knew something Wu did not. The Captain tried not to react, because he knew that he probably wasn't there, but his face betrayed him.

"Captain?" the guard asked.

Wu snapped out of it. "Well done," he droned again, and then he exited as if he had something pressing.

The guards stiffened and saluted, and Wu left without anyone realizing that something was very, very wrong.

CHAPTER 5

The dormitories at the 5-Gen were abysmal. They were crowded, overly so, with men, women, and children, and dark inside. The rooms were all windowless by design, to keep the masses depressed and down.

Steel bunk beds were packed with miserable, malnourished people that barely had the energy to move, let alone the space to do it. It looked like an old tenement building where the poorest of the poor were all living on top of each other in certain squalor.

There were garments strewn on makeshift clotheslines, small hot pots steaming with water for a weak cup of tea. Some people milled about, while others sadly stayed on their bunks due to what seemed like a complete lack of energy to move. The atmosphere was as depressing as depressing can be, aside from some children who didn't seem to know any better. They kicked around a mostly deflated rubber ball, as if nothing were odd about it. They were working with what they had; they would be a part of the dreck that their lot has in this life soon enough. It was remarkable that they hadn't succumbed to the weight of the hopelessness that life was in the 5-Gen.

The gate to the dormitory opened. It was a metal gate that had blocked out the outside lights; when it opened, the population on the inside scattered like cockroaches.

There was more than just the outside gate, of course. The 5-Gen was a prison, after all. There was another wire gate that required keys to gain entry. About twenty officers entered.

"Inspection!" one of the officers yelled.

The guards flowed in with batons out and riot gear on, which was odd because the residents of the dorm were clearly scared into submission.

"On the count!" the officer commanded.

Wu entered as the inhabitants of the dorm scrambled to get on their bunks. Women snatched up errant children, but one escaped and unknowingly waddled into the lion's den. The child stood, in a makeshift cloth diaper of some sort, in front of the lion himself. Wu looked down at the child, and then all around him at the guards who stood ramrod straight and were desperately trying not to look.

"What do we have here?" Wu asked no one in particular.

Wu picked up the errant child, awkwardly, holding him in a way that made it abundantly clear that he wasn't exactly comfortable around kids. The kid wasn't comfortable around Wu either. As if the boy sensed the danger that Wu represented, the child's diaper filled with urine, and it streamed down his leg onto the floor.

Some of the guards eyeballed each other sideways as Wu held the urinating child.

"Who is responsible for this?" Wu looked around expectantly.

An elderly woman, weathered by years of living in horrible conditions, slid off her cot. There was a younger woman on the bunk above her, who looked down nervously as the older woman gingerly moved toward certain consequence.

Wu placed the child on the floor. He stood unsure as to what to do. The old woman, a relative of some sort, went to the child, almost submissively, head bowed, hoping not to be reprimanded, and took the errant boy by the hand.

"Wait!" Wu commanded.

The woman stood still as stone. Wu walked closer to her, his boots clicking in an intimidating way. The woman probably wanted to step out of her own skin and run off, but she did not budge.

"This is your responsibility?" Wu asked.

"This is Pan, my daughter's son. I look after him while she works in the factory."

The tension in the dorm was taut with anxiety. One person who was contributing to the high level of angst was a familiar face. It was Eli, although this version didn't have the white wisp of hair. He watched intently from the top bunk of a bed that was in the same vicinity as the old woman who claimed the urinating boy.

Eli knew he shouldn't act, but he really was fearful of what Wu might do.

"You must be very proud of your daughter. Working in the factory can reap tremendous rewards." Wu paused. "You, however, should be ashamed of the level of care you have for your own responsibilities."

The old woman instinctively stood in front of the boy.

"Please don't punish him; he is just a child."

Wu nodded. "Very true, very true."

Eli jumped off the bunk. He had no idea what would happen, but whatever the Captain had in mind, he knew it couldn't be good.

"The boy *is* just a child, so where would we place the blame for this inexcusable behavior?"

The woman didn't know what to do, but whatever was about to happen, she knew it wasn't going to be good. She managed to push the child off in the direction of some of her other family. The boy toddled off, utterly unaware of the damage he had done and the danger he created. Such was the life of the innocent; they simply had no concept of the consequence of crossing the wicked.

Wu paced in front of the woman. The entire room was filled with anxiety.

"I think that the punishment should fit the crime," Wu said.

"What crime?" the woman asked foolishly.

Wu slapped the woman so hard a tooth was dislodged from her mouth and she fell to the floor. Eli rushed to the woman's side. He wiped her bloodied mouth with a rag.

"What have we here?" Wu asked.

Eli looked up at him defiantly. "She is just an old woman!"

Wu's eyes narrowed. "You are a bold one."

"She can't defend herself!"

"Let me guess—you will defend her?"

"At least I can stand up for myself."

"Perhaps better than an old woman, but truthfully, son, no one under my guard has chance against me, and now I have to make an example of her so that no one else gets any dumb ideas."

"Please, I will take the punishment."

"You would pay for this woman's failure?"

Eli nodded.

"Very well, I will allow it."

Eli helped the woman up and gave her his rag. She looked at him with a combination of gratitude and confusion.

"I am old. Whatever they do to me, it wouldn't leave a scar for long."

"Go back to your cot and rest. Watch the boy," Eli answered.

The woman gently touched Eli on the arm and scuttled off, leaving him to collect her punishment.

Eli looked at Wu. He wasn't afraid, although he probably should have been.

"So, now we can move on to the punishment. Is that okay?" Wu asked sardonically.

"Our dorm is a well maintained one, Captain, I'm not sure there is a need for...."

"It is well maintained, you say? I find that difficult to believe. Did you not just see this child running amok? Urinating all over the floor? You see, there is a puddle of piss right by your feet," Wu said, interrupting.

Eli glanced down. There was a puddle of urine.

"Perhaps if you don't believe me, you should see for yourself."

"I believe you."

"Do you? I feel as if you do not, given your belief as to how well maintained this dormitory is."

Eli sensed that he could not get out of what whatever was going to happen. He had already tested the boundaries by talking back to Wu at all. Now all he could hope for was that he respected him for it.

89

"You see this?" Wu asked Eli, pointing to the puddle of urine the boy left behind.

Eli nodded.

"Come closer. I need you to understand the gravity of the situation."

Eli moved to Wu with trepidation. It was rare that a prisoner got this close to the Captain. It was awkward, to be sure; all the eyes of the dorm were likely on him, without actually appearing to be looking.

"What is your name, prisoner?"

"Eli, sir."

Wu nodded. "It's rare to see a man be so bold as you. I have to say I respect it."

Eli smiled a little, as much as one smiled in a place like this.

"Get on your knees," Wu told him.

The smile disappeared quickly.

"Why are you still standing, prisoner? ON YOUR KNEES!"

Eli got onto his knees.

Wu wore a creepy smile. "Good! Now would you be so kind as to examine the mess?"

Eli looked at the puddle of urine, and then at Wu.

"Go on now, look at it, tell me what you see."

"I don't have to get closer to see that it's urine, sir."

"Hmmm, how can you be sure? Look at it. Get close enough to taste it. In fact, lick it up."

Eli shuddered at the thought. He looked the puddle and back at Wu. Wu still wearing that creepy smile.

"My men can help you, and so can I."

Wu stood in front of Eli, unzipped has pants, and urinated all over him.

CHAPTER 6

Selena lay on a gurney. They had given her a loose cloth smock that made her easily accessible for the poking and prodding. She was there, but she wasn't really there. In her mind she was in another place entirely, with him. She absentmindedly touched the wisp of white that was still dyed into her hair; despite crossing worlds, no barrier could prevent the symbol from staying.

Selena was glad for that. She thought to herself that if the next crossing failed, she would find a way to dye it in this world, although she didn't know how. *It won't matter. I will get back to him.*

It would have been easy for Selena to resent Wu for sending her on a reckless trip across space and time, but she knew that it wasn't a judgment against her; rather, it was a vote of confidence that Selena could stop the other world from crushing the one she hailed from.

It wasn't fair, any of it. The hellish world was being squeezed into a smaller space in the universe by another one. The tears in the fabric of the 5-Gen were small at first, hardly noticeable, in fact. Things had changed; the integrity of the world the 5-Gen sat in was crumbling and causing casualties in both the fabric of the universe as well as human loss.

The fabric of the 5-Gen had been subject to loss of integrity at certain spots. It first started when a prisoner walked into a weak spot in the fabric of the universe. The poor soul was trapped in between the world of the 5-Gen and wherever the other half went in such situations. Other prisoners kept moving, unwilling to help the prisoner, incorrectly assuming that Wu had punished him somehow. The man sat screaming and suffering until finally two guards came and pulled what was left of him free of the break in time and space. When they did, he was very dead, and without legs. It appeared as if a shark on the other side had gnawed at his lower half, killing him slowly. All they could see was blackness from where they pulled the man.

Wu accelerated the science programs to the detriment of other programs, including growing food, the argument being that there might be no one to feed if these holes in the 5-Gen couldn't be patched.

They did find a solution, albeit a temporary one. The 5-Gen scientists came up with a compound to patch the tears in the fabric of their universe, but they warned Wu that it would not hold. A more permanent solution was needed, and while some of these men created the compound to patch holes, others worked on the greater solution.

Selena was struggling with losing a person, but she couldn't imagine losing an entire universe, although it no longer felt like her home, as her heart was where home was, and her heart felt as if it wasn't even in her body. It was with the Theory from the other side, and the longer she was gone from him, the worse the pang of heartache grew. It was hardly bearable.

Yet the idea of her history being pushed into some unknown abyss was still hard to wrap her head around. Selena pushed it out of her mind. She imagined being wrapped up like a pretzel with him, her Theory, far away from this decaying place that would soon be done for.

Finally, the doctors came in for her. Wu came into the room as well, but he and his entourage stayed back, almost not wanting to hear whatever the men of science had to say.

"How are we feeling?" one man asked.

"Normal, fine."

"That a start," the same man said, nodding to another man, who wrote on a clipboard.

"We want to do a full body scan. That means injecting you with a dye and you're having to lie still for about an hour."

"Is that necessary?" she asked.

The doctor looked at Wu.

"We are concerned that crossing over as much as you have could have a degenerative effect on your system."

"Does it matter? He is sending me back anyway."

"For you, no, it doesn't matter. But for others who go after, it might."

"I see. I am a lab rat."

"Pretty much."

"Fine, get on with it."

Wu came over and looked at Selena.

"You are a good soldier in this war for our survival," Wu told Selena.

She nodded as someone injected her with whatever crap they needed to put in her.

"What if you can't figure out how to stop the degradation?" Selena asked Wu.

"In that case, all essential personnel will cross over, just as you have."

"Right—hence the safety tests."

"Correct," Wu told her before they wheeled her off to see how damaged she really was.

She closed her eyes and imagined her Theory. She wondered if he was thinking of her, wondering what happened on the top of that building, not realizing that it was a portal between worlds.

CHAPTER 7

Wu left the medical bay. He didn't want to wait to find out what he already suspected. The scientists had warned him of a molecular denigration before they sent Selena through. Truth was, everything was degenerating anyway—that was the cycle of life—but here at the 5-Gen, things seemed worse than that cycle. Things at the 5-Gen had the cycle of life degenerating at an exponential rate. The fabric of the very universe was becoming a weakened membrane that Wu wouldn't say with any level of confidence would hold, or if it did, for how long.

The same might be said for Selena. The integrity of her body and soul might have been weakened by the crossings as well. Wu thought that she must have hated her time over there with that world's version of his nemesis.

Wu walked in front of his adjunct across the yard. His sense of paranoia grew to the point where he had goose bumps on his arms and legs. He could feel the man lurking, waiting, watching.

The Captain thought he saw the ink-black-haired Theory standing behind a flock of miserable prisoners, but when he stopped and looked further, he could see that no one was actually there.

"Captain?" the adjunct asked.

Wu looked at the man, dazed.

"Everything all right?"

Wu stared at the adjunct as if he were looking right through him, as if he didn't register at all. Wu didn't see anything except for the black-haired Theory that plagued his existence. Wu was able to shut him out sometimes, but now, when he had time to think, was when the man showed up in his mind's eye. The truth was that the black Theory was both. He was there and he was not. Wu's obsession had him seeing Theory pop up everywhere in the compound. Mostly he saw him in the mirror in his office, behind him, talking, taunting, but when Wu would turn around, he was gone.

Wu was concerned that he was losing his mind—or perhaps it was the space in his head that was degrading like the membrane in the universe.

"Leave me," Wu finally managed to order his subordinate.

The adjunct nodded, saluted, and the hustled off in the opposite direction, most likely relieved that he could be excused by the increasingly odd and disturbing behavior of his superior.

Wu took a deep breath and looked to see that his nemesis, real or imagined, was also gone. The Captain walked briskly to his austere office. Once inside, he took off his hat, which made him look substantially taller—by design, of course. His father and grandfather before him were both short as well, and they did whatever they could to seem larger than life.

He wasn't larger than life; it was nothing more than a façade. Wu was constantly suffering under his mask of control and command. The Captain wondered if somehow his father and grandfather suffered the same silent fate. They must have been better at hiding it, Wu thought as he looked at the black-and-white photographs that hung on the walls of his office. In the images, his father and grandfather stood ramrod straight with other officers; some gaunt and pathetic-looking prisoners seemed unaware that they had been captured by the imagery, whereas their captors were proud of the state in which they were seen and kept.

"They can't help you now." The voice came from what seemed like all over the room.

Wu knew not to turn. *It isn't real; it can't be.*

"My ancestors inspire me. I would think you would know that," Wu responded.

The male voice sniggered at Wu, who looked in the mirror and saw the full head of black hair attached to his nemesis, his Theory. He sat at his desk, feet up on it, clearly not afraid.

"That's total bullshit. You are falling apart, just like your world. You are desperate for answers that you will never have."

"I have answers; you just don't know about them."

Theory scoffed at Wu, "I know everything about you and this place. It is you who don't know jack."

A bead of sweat began to form at Wu's temple. "What do you want?"

"That is the one thing that you *do* know. I want you and this world to die."

Wu turned around in rage, but the man whom he imagined to be there, was not. The man alone in the room wanted to scream, but he knew that he could not, for to do so would to be to alert the inmates and guards that he was indeed in crisis, and that he was no longer fit to lead.

The Captain wiped the sweat from his forehead and went to his liquor cabinet. He rarely drank, but these days it seemed that he was taking a nip here and there to get himself through the days.

Wu's hand shook as he poured the clear but powerful liquid into a tin cup that he used for making weak tea from the same bag over and over again. He poured himself half a mug and downed it quickly, his throat on fire. Then he poured another.

CHAPTER 8

Eli couldn't get the taste of urine out of his mouth no matter how much he rinsed it. He was lucky to have some filtered water; that wasn't always the case. Sometimes there was no water at all.

This was the land of the dead or dying. Hell was proud to call this home—even without the flames, this place was hot with tortured souls.

"There is a place out there somewhere that is full of hope." The voice came from behind Eli.

He turned and saw Simeon. This was the one person that could really pass for a friend. Friends were hard to come by in the 5-Gen. They really didn't exist. It was sort of every man for him/herself. Survival was the name of the game, even though so many times no one really wanted to play.

"It's hard to be hopeful when you can't shake the taste of urine from your mouth."

"Try this," Simeon suggested, handing him a leaf.

"What is it?"

"Poison, to put you out of your misery—also me out of mine."

Eli didn't know whether to believe him or not. He often couldn't read Simeon.

"Just trust me. It's called mint."

"You grew it? Here? Nothing grows here," Eli said.

"Nope, it's from the other side. I've been saving it."

"It's not true. It can't be."

Simeon placed a hand on Eli's shoulder. He knew he had been utterly demoralized—such a thing was easy in a place like this. What was not easy was to rebound from such demoralization, but Simeon tried, regardless. He had known the despair of 5-Gen life all too well himself.

"It is true. He has told me. This is proof. Take it," Simeon suggested, holding the leaf.

Eli took it. He studied it in certain wonder. It must be true, because nothing really grew in the 5-Gen. It was as if the color green didn't exist in this world—everything was dead.

Simeon took a small bite of the leaf. Eli watched as his friend chewed slowly, as he savored whatever gift his mouth had received. Finally, emboldened by example, he did the same. The flush of freshness cleared his mind of the taste he could not shake previously. It was a wonder of the senses.

Simeon saw the bliss in Eli. It was a rare moment, but also an opportunity to recruit him to the cause. Stories existed about another place, one that wasn't all misery all the time. Most of the denizens of the 5-Gen would settle for an occasional happiness after living through the hell that was daily life—perhaps that was true of any existence, but it was exponentially true of this one.

"Better, right?"

Eli nodded, as his senses were through the roof with stimulation.

"This is what we can partake of on the other side—so many wonders. Theory has told me, but he needs our help."

Eli chewed his leaf, savoring every incredible burst of flavor. It was euphoric, but even in the midst of the high, he was concerned about what was being asked of him.

"I dunno, Simeon. You see what they just did to me, right? And to be honest, I think we got off lightly. I'm pretty sure they were thinking of killing that baby."

Simeon placed a hand on Eli's shoulder. Trying to recruit when the base of the population was so beaten down was no simple task, but this was also the key to turning the tide. This was how to balance the imbalance of what this hell was all too used to being.

"I did see, we all did. But that is precisely why we need to act. Theory is changing things, and we must support that change. Imagine when this hell hole becomes a 6-Gen? Or 7? That would mean more suffering at the behest of whatever asshole takes over for the Captain."

Eli knew that on some level Simeon was right, yet he still debated as to how he could make a difference. Inside him somewhere he possessed the temerity to fight for what he believed in, yet recent events seemed to show him that the fight might not be winnable.

"What do you want me to do?" Eli asked.

"For now, let's get you rested. Tomorrow is a new day, full of hope!"

Eli nodded out of gratitude, both for not having to get back on the front line, but also for the fact he had a friend—even if he was the only one; the notion that he wasn't alone provided strength Eli didn't even know he had.

CHAPTER 9

Selena couldn't wait to leave; even though the leaving might kill her. Staying might make her kill herself. She was lying on a barracks cot, alone and sequestered. Selena realized that she had become a prisoner at the 5-Gen. All of a sudden, the tables had turned, and the weight of misery was upon her. Even being a guard at the prison was miserable, but prisoner status was 1000% worse.

Selena imagined being in Theory's arms, wrapped like two halves of a pretzel that no matter how you twisted them, they always fit together. The thought warmed her soul. She had never had chemistry with anyone like this—of course, romance wasn't exactly commonplace in hell. Perhaps it wasn't common anywhere. Regardless, Selena knew that what she had experienced with the other Theory was not commonplace anywhere in any space or in any time. What they had was one of a kind, in any universe. Selena was sure of it.

When she was with him, it was as if all equilibrium had been restored in her orbit. Theory had the ability to see into Selena's soul, and she could see into his. At first, she thought she had experienced some sort of effect of the crossing, that she was soon to have an aneurism, or maybe it was a tumor that was sitting on her brain and spinal cord.

Selena knew she was in trouble the moment they first touched. Like a jump start to revitalize a car, Theory's touch had reignited her long since dead soul, but now it felt like she was dead all over again. It seemed that her inner fire had been doused and the only way to rekindle it was to be one with Theory, again. It was utterly soul-breaking to not only be separated from her person but to be in such a state that the rules of conventional space and time couldn't be applied. The attempt to return, if not properly executed, could kill her—not that she minded that notion. Death seemed to be a welcome notion if Selena couldn't be back with Theory, or even worse, if she were stuck in the 5-Gen. Once you have escaped living amongst the dead, as it turns out, you aren't so keen on returning to such unfortunate circumstances.

Selena tried desperately to sleep, but as hard as she tried, her mind raced with all that could go wrong or was going wrong. Her heart felt like it might pound out of her chest. It was odd for her; she knew more than anything else that she wanted to be in the other world, with *that* Theory, but at the same time she was anxious as to how things would work out here. The move to another universe wasn't like moving in with a boyfriend; this time, she would have to stay. What if didn't work out? What should she do then? Relationships at the 5-Gen were few and far between, for guards and prisoners alike. Selena had limited involvement with everyone, but Theory changed all that. She questioned her inexperience and the difference in worlds as the cause of her fall for his seduction. This was a major fuck-up. She was supposed to go over and eliminate him, but instead she was going to love him for as long as he would allow it. Selena promised herself that she had to try to make this work, despite any consequence to herself or her standing in this world. She was going to defect, full on, whether it worked or not.

Selena practically jumped off the cot when the door opened suddenly. Wu entered with one of the men who had examined her and run tests. She stood, confused and disoriented; something must be wrong for them to come.

"Everything OK, Captain?" Selena asked.

"We have the results of your tests," Wu stated ominously.

Selena looked at the man who had accompanied Wu. He averted his gaze. She knew that couldn't be good news.

"Go on, Burns, tell her."

Burns was a slight man, with a narrow face like a rodent. He remained silent for a moment, his gaze still averted from Selena's eyes. Finally, he opened the file chart that he carried with him.

"As you know, we ran a battery of tests before you crossed initially, to make sure you were suitable for the crossing, but also to have a baseline for comparison if we ever had an opportunity to test you again. That opportunity presented itself when you returned."

"Yes, I understand."

"When we did the comparison, we did find some differences."

"You going to tell me what they are?" Selena asked nervously.

"It appears that you have tumors growing on your brain. While we can't be 100% certain that is a direct result of the crossing, we are guessing it is. Too small amount of time has gone by to see tumors of this size."

"I was gone for two years. Seems like a long enough time for anything."

Burns looked at Wu.

"You were gone for two months for us—we expect that the difference in time/space has compromised your health," Burns said.

"So, if I go back, I may be healthy again?"

"It is possible. You would have to get checked there to be sure, but there is another concern."

"What's that?"

Burns sighed. "The crossing could kill you before you get there."

"I understand. What are my options?"

"Since you have a new objective that involves a crossing, we feel like you should wait until you return before we treat it."

"What's the treatment?"

"Surgery, followed by radiation. It will be intense; the nature of these tumors is an aggressive one."

Selena looked at Wu. "Yes, of course, after the mission is a success."

Wu had that creepy little smile run across his thin lips. "You can leave us," he told the doctor.

The man nodded at Selena, most likely from admiration. Wu had told him that she would put duty first and foremost. The doctor had been skeptical but clearly had been proven wrong.

When the man of science left, Wu stood in silence briefly. "I told him you would honor duty."

"Of course, it is my honor to have been selected for such an important mission, Captain."

"There is no one else I could have trusted, Theory must die in both worlds for ours to survive," Wu stated.

"I couldn't agree more."

"We will take care of you as soon as the mission is successful," Wu said, patting Selena on her shoulder.

It was an act. Wu couldn't even properly fake tenderness without a condition put on it at some point. Selena was more resolved than ever to get back to her person. She knew that she would rather spend the rest of her life with him, even if she had little to none of it left.

CHAPTER 10

Wu walked briskly, kicking up the grey dust of the 5-Gen. He wasn't sure if it was the lack of sleep or paranoia that had him seeing the black-haired Theory behind every corner, hearing his voice taunt him. It was probably both.

When the world you are responsible for is collapsing under the weight of an invader, you feel responsible. Wu's lineage had been commanding the 5-Gen successfully since the beginning of recorded time. The weight of all his ancestors' disappointment was crushing him, even to the point where he was willfully killing his most trusted lieutenant. He didn't care. All that mattered was surviving, even if Selena died. Wu's honor, and the integrity of the world he lived in, were both at stake.

He was falling apart, and he knew it. Wu questioned his own ability despite the fact that this was his birthright and this was what he was bred to do. He was failing, nonetheless. Wu rode himself—he was pathetic, worthless, and ineffective; his father and grandfather, if either were alive, would have him hanged and fix this like a real commander.

Wu stopped when he heard the screaming. When he looked around, he saw that one of the prisoners had fallen into a hole, and the others where frantically trying to get him out. Guards beat the prisoners trying to help the man, getting them away from his arms flailing wildly. That was when Wu saw him, Theory, standing behind all the action, smiling at Wu as if he knew something Wu didn't.

Wu went over to see that the man hadn't fallen in a hole, at least not a conventional one—this was a tear in the fabric of the universe. The man was wailing in obvious pain. Wu kicked him in the face violently and some of the other guards joined in until the man was unconscious.

"This isn't safe, Captain. We will get him out," a guard suggested.

"Leave him in there; it will plug the hole," Wu instructed.

"Sir, he is still alive. He will be screaming and making the other inmates agitated."

"Then I suggest you change his status and notify his family of his demise."

The guards looked at Wu, wondering for a moment whether he could be serious, but that stern, focused, reptilian stare answered their questions and three of them unholstered their batons and beat the man until he was dead. Wu walked away, as the inmates who could bear to watch vomited from the blood and brains that were sprayed about the grey dirt in the yard.

Wu stopped and looked at the inmates that were sickened by what they were witnessing, and screamed at them, "Get back to work!"

Wu stormed off, but soon found he wasn't walking alone, even though he was. The black-haired Theory, obviously a figment of his imagination, taunted him from the depths of his own mind.

"You aren't really here," Wu stated, looking at the man next to him.

"Is that what you are telling yourself?" black-haired Theory quipped.

Wu looked forward, as if he believed that if he didn't acknowledge Theory, he would somehow go away.

"I *am* here. In fact, I am everywhere, Captain, and there isn't shit you can do about it."

Wu tried to avert his eyes, keenly aware that to an outsider looking at him, he must seem mad. Inside, he was boiling. He stopped, and Theory did too. Wu stuck a jabbed finger in Theory's face.

"You aren't here! You aren't anywhere!"

Theory wore a shit-eating grin. "Look at that!" Theory pointed to the dead man slumped.

Wu picked up his pace and refused to look at the dead man who plugged a hole in the universe.

"Even if you don't acknowledge me or what I am doing to your world, it doesn't mean I don't exist. You get that, right?" Theory asked Wu.

Wu stared at Theory. He seemed as if he were really there, standing in front of him. Wu tried to look through him, but he couldn't. In his mind, the Captain rationalized that the lack of sleep and the stress were playing tricks on him. Nevertheless, he reached out as if to touch his imaginary nemesis, and found out. He wasn't imaginary at all.

He was really there.

Blackness enveloped the Captain. He passed out, and lay on the ground briefly before anyone noticed. His nemesis ran off, disappearing as seamlessly as he had appeared, like a ghost.

CHAPTER 11

Eli was nervous. He sat on his bunk, trying to ignore the putrid smell that came from the bunk below. It was difficult to disregard. The smell exacerbated the anxiety he was feeling. He wanted to help Simeon and Theory. The promise of a better life, even if it was just a little better, was enough to motivate him into service. The 5-Gen was a place thick with misery, so much so that at times it didn't feel manageable. This was death, or worse—knowing you would die and in pain, with immeasurable suffering, yet unable to find the relief of the reaper.

Theory was a myth. Only a few people had ever seen him, and the prison itself never acknowledged his existence. But this myth was growing in the dorms, propagated by a select few like Simeon, and their ranks were growing.

Eli was no exception. He was still grateful for the leaf that removed the taste of piss from his mouth, but it was uplifting as well, as if he had chewed on hope. Part of him was excited to do something that might change the generational misery, but then part of him was scared to death as to what would happen if he failed or the movement failed. So, he sat in the stench and wondered if he could survive whatever lay ahead of him, or if it even mattered.

Eli knew Simeon would return after the prisoner count, but until then everyone remained on their bunks where they could be accounted for. He looked around wondering who else might be in on whatever Theory had in mind to liberate the 5-Gen.

It all seemed as it had been, prisoners overpowered for days, weeks, years, beaten down physically and mentally into submission and depression so deep that it felt like it never could be overcome. It was easy for Eli to feel like that, but to have tasted hope—that changed things. If only there were a way for all the prisoners to have hope! But Eli doubted that there was a realistic way for that to happen. He had tasted the other world, where that hope was born and bred, and he barely could suppress the fear of what might happen if he rebelled.

Then Eli saw something out of the corner of his eye. It was movement. When he looked again, whatever he saw had disappeared. He scanned the room again. Eli had a good view, as his bunk was somewhat centrally located, and high up, like a watchtower at the center of his shitty little universe.

He looked. It was as if everyone were staring at him. The room rotated around on Eli. The shadow that he had seen earlier spun like smoke, in circles. It finally took a form facing him sitting on his bunk. Except his bunk wasn't a bunk anymore. At least, the dorm had faded away to blackness, as if Eli were in a car driving away from that reality toward wherever he was headed.

The blackness of the dorm flew away. Eli was enveloped in darkness as the small amount of light that had been the dorm became smaller and smaller until the little dot was reduced to nothingness. It was beyond disorienting. Then came an ambient sound, like the sound of whale song. It was meditative, which must have been the objective, as Eli was able to relax from the intensity of the anxiety.

Eli closed his eyes. A wave of calmness washed over him.

"You can open your eyes now, Eli. You have arrived."

Eli did open his eyes. He found himself standing in a white room with windows all around. Outside, there were stars that oozed out of the blackness. There were so many, like lights dotted about the blackness, almost decorative. It was so breathtaking that Eli almost forgot he wasn't alone.

"Beautiful, isn't it?"

Eli turned to see Simeon. He was dressed in the same loose-fitting uniform of the 5-Gen, except the garment was white instead of the faded grey.

Eli nodded. Simeon smiled.

"You have questions, I'm sure."

"Where are we?" Elis asked.

"This is a safe room of sorts, a place where we can meet and discuss things freely."

"How did I get here?"

Simeon smiled. "I thought you would know."

Eli was about to tell Simeon that he did not know, when two opaque shadows from opposite ends of the room converged, and when they did, they formed a single man.

"What the fuck?"

"Ha! I've never heard you swear," Simeon chuckled.

Eli wasn't laughing. He had just seen a man materialize out of two converging opaque shadows. The man extended his hand to Simeon. They shook, but it soon became a hug. They were obviously familiar. The men broke the embrace and looked at Eli, who stood befuddled to the gills.

"Shit, Eli. This is Elysium Theory, our benefactor."

Theory smiled and extended both arms, embracing Eli as if he were an old friend. "Good to finally meet this version of you."

Eli broke the embrace and looked to Simeon for answers.

"I haven't explained that far ahead, Theory."

"What is he talking about? This version? And where the hell are we?"

"I understand. You have a lot of questions—understandably so," Theory assured Eli.

"Where are we?"

"A place between space and time, and then some."

"And how did I get here? Like you did?" Eli asked his host.

"No, you and Simeon had some help. I have a unique ability to travel here without the benefit of a boost."

"The mint," Simeon explained, "has hallucinogenic properties."

"This is a hallucination? Feels real to me."

"It may, but I assure you, right now you are tripping balls."

"The leaf allows you to free your mind and tune to a particular frequency," Theory explained.

"You and Simeon are on the same trip?"

"You and Simeon are. I don't require the leaf to be here, but we haven't the time. We need your help, Eli. We were hoping that you agreed with our goals of being free of the 5-Gen. It's a form of hell, you know."

"Free of it how?" Eli asked.

"You have seen things happening there, no? Strange things? Rips in the fabric of the universe?"

Eli looked at Simeon, who nodded at him.

"Yeah, I've seen people lose limbs in whatever that is."

"That is me, trying to free the people who suffer."

"That's you? People have died from those rips."

"Death is a form of freedom, Eli," Theory defended. "Besides, in war inevitability there are casualties."

"Let me get this right—you drugged me to get me here in order to recruit me for your war?"

"Well, when you say it like that…."

"Eli, we can be free, live in another world. It isn't like what we have known," Simeon added.

"We are all going? Everyone?"

"That's the idea. Everyone, guards included. Even Wu, if he survives." Theory said, "I doubt it will be without casualties. In fact, there will be loss, but for those who survive the journey, it will be as if the dead were alive again."

Eli was both alive with excitement and dead with fear at the same time. Finally, he asked, "What is it that you want me to do?"

Theory smiled. "The fabric of the 5-Gen is degenerating. The other universe is overpowering it—by design, of course. There will be a bridge that appears at some point soon. I am not sure where on the 5-Gen, or even exactly when, but when the time comes, I will need you boys to guide the lost souls through the passage."

"We will get to be free together," Simeon added.

"The guards, the Captain, they will just lock down the facility if there is an escape in progress."

Theory nodded. "No one has escaped the 5-Gen, except me, but I don't actually exist in that world—just a facsimile."

Eli grabbed his head.

"It's a side effect of the hallucinogen," Simeon explained

"You haven't much time, but I am glad you came, and that you see the value in helping your fellow prisoners. You will be a hero when this is all said and done."

"I have no training, Mr. Theory. I was born a prisoner. I don't feel qualified for this. You refer to this as a war, but I am no soldier."

"I understand the trepidation. There is much uncertainty, and much to lose, but I assure you that on the other side, there is a life worth living and dying for, but you have to make that choice. The truth is that I am going to crush Wu's hell with or without you, but the survival of the people within those prison walls rests solely on you boys."

Eli's headache was worse. He wasn't sure if it was the effect of the drug wearing off or the pressure of the concept of destroying the only life he had ever known for parts unknown. What if it were a trick? Eli looked at Theory. His mouth was moving, yet the words were incomprehensible. Then, just like he arrived, he was enveloped in blackness. The car pulled away from the light, and soon he was back where he had started, or had been all along, on his bunk, smelling the putrid stench that came from below.

CHAPTER 12

Selena knew there was something wrong. She felt off, filled with something that was a foreign invader. It was a bizarre sensation. Perhaps it was the testing they had done on her that had created an anxiety that would otherwise not have been there, or perhaps it was something else entirely.

She lay there on that lonely cot, in an empty garrison. Selena felt like she might be sick. A wave of nausea came over her and she doubled over. Sweat began to form on her head, and with the feeling of sickness came an intense anxiety as well.

Selena was sore, too. What was happening? Was this the stress of the travel? She got up. She assumed she wasn't supposed to leave the barracks, but no one told her not to, either.

Going outside was what Selena needed. The air, while not the best quality, was better than the limited ventilation that housing provided. Her head still pounded, but the nausea abated a bit.

Selena walked with purpose but no direction. She was reminded of the hell that the 5-Gen was—prisoners labored, moving rocks for no particular reason, restringing the noose on the gallows for the next of their brethren to get a public death. Some swept dust. When she was a guard, before she had become an agent provocateur, Selena didn't notice what these wretched people were going through, yet somehow the trip through space time changed all that. It was as if she were an empath, like she could feel the weight of the despair.

There were disturbing images beyond the misery of the prisoners. The guards were also miserable, because despite being on the right side of the dynamic with in the 5-Gen, they were prisoners too. They lived their lives within these walls and called this living hell home, just as the inmates did.

Still, that wasn't it. The situation had become dire. There was more and more of the red compound used to patch holes. Some of it was for small areas, but some areas were much larger, with people trapped within the confines of the compound. They were frozen in time, or perhaps dead; maybe it was a purgatory of sorts. Selena wondered if they would come back to life if the compound melted away somehow.

Selena stopped and looked at the people trapped in the compound. She lingered there, deeply affected by their stasis, if it was even that—yet she noticed that the other inhabitants didn't seem to register that these people were even there. Like an art installment that the locals have seen redundantly, no one saw what Selena saw, or they didn't want to.

The yard was littered with other instances of holes in the 5-Gen being plugged. Half a man was being covered in the compound by guards, as if they were watering a garden. The man looked as if he had been cut in half and left there, as if in some horror movie or haunted house. Soon the man was covered in the compound, and he was just another installment for the population to pretend wasn't there.

A wave of heavy nausea came over Selena, and she doubled over. She thought she would be sick, but even she was distracted by the screams of a woman. She looked up to see the woman—she was scared shitless and screaming as the prisoners tried to avoid her and the guards attempted to catch her.

The woman was like a headless chicken, except this chicken wore a white tunic, definitely not of the 5-Gen world. Selena got herself up, knowing that if what she suspected were true, she was the only one qualified to deal with this situation. This woman had somehow crossed over.

Guards and prisoners were both engaged by this odd visitor. The prisoners were afraid, and clearly the guards shared their trepidation, but they tried to catch her, making the chicken that much more frantic.

"Hey!" Selena yelled, "Fall back—I got this."

The guards looked at Selena, almost grateful to be relieved of the latest round of chaos. The semicircle they had formed to try to ensnare the woman disbanded much faster than it had formed. Once the guards were no longer distracted, the prisoners feigned getting back to their labors, but watched intently out of the corner of their eyes.

Selena approached the woman, hands in the air, showing that she meant no harm. She maintained eye contact, trying to get the stranger to focus on her.

"My name is Selena. What's your name?'

Despite the fact the woman was being spoken to, the distress threw her; she was utterly befuddled, looking around, still unsuccessfully trying to get her bearings.

Selena approached slowly, hands raised, speaking in a calm, even voice. "I know you must be frightened, but no one will hurt you. What is your name?"

The woman was shaking, but she seemed to settle a little. She stared at Selena, as if she knew she was speaking to her, yet could not see or hear. She backed up, and backed up again, until she bumped into the half of a man that had been sealed in fresh compound. She looked and saw the horror-movie-like image and screamed.

Selena got to her and held her, and instinctively the woman latched on like a desperate barnacle.

"It's OK. I got you; you are going to be OK," Selena whispered gently as she stroked the stranger's hair.

A crowd by now had formed, curious to see what would happen next. It was mostly guards, but there were prisoners mixed into the maelstrom who stole furtive glances at what was going on, wondering silently if this development was a cause for hope or just more fear. The truth was, they felt a tinge of both.

The crowd quickly pretended to forget about the two women who held each other in the grey dirt yard as they returned to their slavish work. Captain Wu split the crowd as he made his way through the mass of gawkers.

"What is this?" Wu asked, looking at Selena.

"She is from the other side, Captain, and if they have figured out how to send one, others will surely follow. The war you started has just escalated."

"Get everyone back—lock down the facility," Wu commanded his Adjunct.

The guards sprang into action, herding the prisoners to their dorms, leaving Wu and his adjunct standing there, looking at Selena and the stranger she protected, wrapped in her arms.

"You used to be a top interrogator, Selena; now look at you," Wu said

"She is frightened, Captain, the subject of an experiment. Someone tossed her off a cliff or tall building at a spot that bridges our worlds, just like you did with me."

Wu looked at Selena with fury in his eyes. He turned to his adjunct and commanded him to get more guards, and he ran off.

"What do you suggest I do, since you seem to be the expert on these matters?" Wu asked.

"She knows nothing. She is the subject of an experiment, nothing more."

"As you deftly pointed out, you were also the subject of a similar experiment, and you know quite a bit."

Four guards came running and looked to their Captain.

"Take her."

The men brutally separated Selena and her ward. The woman bucked and screamed, until she was punched violently in her face, knocking her unconscious. The guards carried her away.

"Get ready," Wu told Selena. "Carry out your mission; kill him before he crushes our world."

"What if killing him doesn't work?"

"How can it not? He is behind this, I see." Wu caught himself.

Selena's eyes narrowed. "You see what?"

"It's unimportant. What matters is that you make the journey, and you execute the objective."

Selena got up off the ground and dusted herself off. She stood before Wu and nodded. "I'm ready."

PART THREE

CHAPTER 1

Theory woke up on the floor. He had dreamt of Simeon and Eli and himself. In the dream it was him, but also not quite him—a bizarre sensation, to be sure.

He got himself off the floor, albeit barely; his drug and alcohol consumption had increased exponentially. He knew he was filling a void, or trying to in a stupid and immature way, although these realizations always came in the aftermath, when the consequences were rearing their ugly, Medusa-like heads.

Theory looked at his home. He had made a mess of it in his drug-induced haze. He would have the service come and make it go away—he would try to work, although that merely consisted of trying to find the cosmic door his soulmate had gone through, and pass that off as whatever he needed it to look like.

They had the debacles at the building explained off as cult suicides, but the issue was that they were at the same building, at the same time, as they had to recreate the circumstances of how Selena disappeared. Simeon had been warning him that the Black Syndicate would come, and they had. Since then, the experiments had ground to a halt, but Theory knew that he could not give up—nothing was more worth fighting for, regardless of consequences. He would have to get back to it, somehow, some way. He needed to reunite with Her. Period.

There came a knock at the door. Theory wasn't in the mood to see or deal with anyone, so he didn't answer. Another knock. Theory wondered if they had finally come to collect him for his misdeeds, but the tenor of the knock wasn't forceful—it was probing.

Finally, Theory heard keys jingling, and then the door opening. He went into the shower before he could find out who it was.

The hot water hitting his back was a brief respite. She came to him in his imagination—or was it a hallucination from too many drugs and too little sleep? But for Theory, she was there; he could feel her arms wrapped around his crumbling soul, and for a moment he stopped depreciating and had some semblance of living.

"I've missed you," she whispered in his ear.

Theory closed his eyes in certain bliss. When she told him how she felt, it melted his previously icy heart and warmed him with a comfort that he had not felt for a long time.

"I need to see you," Theory pleaded.

"You will, soon, my love, I promise."

He felt her arms slip away, but took stock of her touch as they did, savoring every last imaginary second of it. Theory wished he could drown in the shower. She was gone, passed into another world, and deep down he feared he would never get her back. It left a wound on his psyche that he thought would never heal, but something told him not to give up. His mind wouldn't let him, despite his covert attempts to finish himself with enough drugs and alcohol to kill a small mammoth. No, Theory told himself, he must persist; she was coming back … some way, somehow, she was. He let the hot water hit his aching, hungover body, knowing that his assistants were waiting for him to do something productive for a change. Finally, he shut off the water and dried off, ready to face things sober.

Theory wiped the steam from the mirror and stared. He looked like hell, and he knew it.

"What the fuck are you doing?"

It wasn't the first time he had asked himself that, and being the addict that he was, it most likely wasn't the last. The habit he needed to feed was that of love—Selena was the one drug that could keep him away from all the others. He made the promise to himself that he would stop with the coke, the booze, the prostitutes, and he actually believed that he would, but time and time again Theory, like all addicts before him, would need to fill that hole filled with emptiness that could be only temporarily staved off with more potent fare, usually lots of it. This time would be different. It had to be.

When he went back into the living room area, Simeon was there. He had the crew already in place to erase all evidence of his latest effort to assuage his pain.

"I made coffee," Simeon stated. "Perhaps we can take some on the deck?"

Theory nodded. He realized that Simeon was enabling him; the poor kid actually believed he was helping. Simeon went to the kitchen and Theory went to the balcony. His views were incredible. He was so high up; it amazed him that he hadn't fallen off in one of his substance-abuse-filled nights. The clean-up crew hadn't gotten outside yet, and even though Theory couldn't remember being outside, the evidence showed otherwise. There were a few empty bottles strewn about, a glass with lipstick on it. He didn't remember guests, either. Theory knew that he had taken this too far, but what he didn't know was whether he could ever climb his way out of the deep hole he had dug for himself.

Simeon came out to the deck with two steaming cups of coffee. Theory's stomach was sour, as was always the case when he had overindulged. The coffee might make it worse, but it could also help alleviate his pounding headache. Theory took the mug that Simeon offered. He sipped it gratefully.

"I think we should get back to work. Our sponsors are getting antsy," Simeon suggested.

"Yes, that makes sense."

Relief washed over Simeon's face. They had not produced original content in several months.

"We should go into the office and listen to pitches," Theory added.

"I have one right now, if you are interested."

Theory took another sip of his coffee and nodded. Simeon placed his coffee down and went back inside. When he came back he had an envelope, which he handed to Theory.

Theory sipped his coffee and sat down. He put the mug on the table and opened the envelope. He pulled out a grainy photograph. It was of legs, half a body's legs.

"What the fuck is this?"

"Excellent question—appeared out of nowhere."

"And the rest of the body?" Theory asked.

"That was all of it."

"And how is this a show?"

"The location where the legs materialized, I think, would answer that for you."

Theory looked at Simeon. "The building? Selena's building?"

Simeon nodded.

"Holy shit!"

"Holy shit indeed. But that's not the end of the story; there's more."

Theory pulled out another photograph, it was of two bodies on the slab, next to each other. One was just the legs, but one was a full body. The odd thing was that they had the same tattoo on the left quad and the same birthmark on the right.

"What is this? Identical twins that got the same tattoo?" Theory asked.

"They are the same person, Elysium. They both died at the same time, but in different places. The legs here probably got caught in between somewhere, but apparently when he died, so did his match from our side."

"They are the same person? Are you certain?"

"I am. This is your story."

Theory's story was about Selena. That's what was spinning in his head. While not definitive, this seemed to be proof that there was, as he had suspected, a parallel universe, where the same people that existed there, existed here. What wasn't clear was why the worlds were inexplicably connected. In theory, worlds should be able to exist without one affecting the other—*why would this be?*

"Where do we start? The building? Maybe something we did caused this?" Theory asked.

"I don't think so. I am afraid the only thing we may have done is kill the matches from the other side when we tossed their counterparts off the building." Simeon paused. We should start at the morgue. The building doesn't matter—in fact, we probably should stay completely away from there unless we want to incur the wrath of the Black Syndicate. They have a big boner for you, if you haven't noticed."

Theory nodded solemnly. He was sure that Simeon knew he wanted to live by that building. No one understood why, but the way between worlds was for some reason there.

"Let's make a show."

"The sponsors will be thrilled, Theory, and so will your legions of fans. You're back!" Simeon patted his boss' back like he was a dog who had just behaved well.

Theory sipped his coffee. He heard Selena whisper to him. He knew that he would have to find another way to stave off his obsession. Simeon had given him that way.

CHAPTER 2

Selena and Major Ott stood staring. They exchanged looks with each other, and then resumed staring forward. The room they were in was a white brick; there was nothing on the walls, the room was sterile.

They had been staring because what they were looking at seemed impossible, even to them. There were sets of people—some appeared to be exact copies, though some, like the sole set of legs, clearly were not quite discernible as matches.

"The people in the grey shirts and pants are from the other side, we suspect that they died there, causing their counterparts to die here," Selena told her superior.

"Why is this happening now? And why are bodies from their side ending up on ours?"

"The working hypothesis is that the worlds are somehow more connected now, thus having that effect. We assume they have had bodies on their side show up from ours too. The interesting part is that they seem to all show up around the same building where we were having jumpers."

"What does that even mean?"

"I think that is a soft spot of sorts between worlds, Major."

"What do you suggest we do?"

"If we can, I think we need to find a way to build a bridge. It seems we are getting only half the story. If we could have all of it, we might be able to stop this madness."

"You want to transverse worlds? Given the bodies piling up, I am not sure that is such a great idea."

"That's precisely why we need to do it, Major, if we can. I need your authorization for the funds—this won't be cheap—but at this point I don't see what choice we have. Lives are being lost on both ends, and it seems as if whatever gap exists between universes is narrowing significantly, to the point where one or both may collapse in on each other. This is uncharted territory. I think it would be wholly irresponsible not to have the full weight of syndicate resources behind this project."

Ott looked at the pairs of bodies lined up. "This goes higher up than me, Selena, but I will grant provisional approval while I convince upstairs."

"Thank you, sir."

"Figure this out, Selena, and fast—of all the shit I've seen over the years, this makes me the most nervous of all." He placed a hand on Selena's back and then left.

Selena stared at the bodies for some time, as if the answer might rise out of them magically, but when none did, she left the morgue too. She knew she had to, as she had allowed Simeon access so that he could distract Theory from the building she was about to put under lockdown. She couldn't have him tossing people off the skyscraper anymore; she needed the building for her own experiments. Selena wondered if her counterpart on the other side was thinking the same thing and they would each build part of the bridge and then meet in the middle. Little did she know that her other wasn't on that side anymore.

She was already here.

CHAPTER 3

Eli waited in the office, just like Simeon told him. The idea was that somehow he would get Theory back to work, and therefore save their jobs, although it was also clear that Simeon and he both had ideas of taking over for Theory, eventually running the show together as a couple, without the insanity that had been keeping the show off track.

Simeon insisted that they needed to show that they could lead Theory back into the fold and then nudge him out. The investors would need to see that they were able, and beyond capable.

Eli wanted to believe in Simeon, although something told him that he shouldn't. He had always thought that Simeon saw him as a rival, but Simeon assured him that wasn't the case, more that he was intimidated by his skill. The irony was that Eli had felt the same about Simeon.

Things changed when they started having a relationship. It was mostly sexual in nature; Simeon didn't seem capable of much beyond sex, and Eli wasn't sure if he was either, but still chose to put the onus on Simeon. The truth was that Eli enjoyed the sex, and the exchange. Both were career men who really didn't have time to be distracted by emotions, but Eli was still feeling them despite himself. He wondered—or was it hoped—that Simeon did too

Eli was alone in the office. There were fewer and fewer staff on hand since the productions had tapered off. It had been months since there had been an original Theory show to air, let alone be produced. Sure, they rolled out the cameras and the sound; they even had production assistants and extras to give the illusion of something being done, but all that was happening was experiments, and those had not been successful in the least. It was a wonder that they had not been shut down for good, and all arrested for their actions. Something or someone was protecting them—had to be—but who?

Eli had been waiting for hours. In all fairness, he had arrived early, but Simeon was also late. Eli paced. He didn't know what else to do. He was startled by the sound of the elevator opening, which was odd, since he was in fact waiting for them to arrive. Except it wasn't who he had expected at all.

Selena Black came off the lift alone. She had a confident stride, almost like a runway model who knew how attractive she was in the eyes of her audience. Eli couldn't help but ogle her as she came toward him. It was a sharp contrast to how he had behaved the last time he saw her, although she hadn't seen him—or so he thought.

"Not hiding under a desk this time?"

"You knew I was there?"

"You know who I work for, I assume? We don't enter a room without knowing who is in it."

"You didn't take me in—why?"

"We weren't interested in you. Your boyfriend, on the other hand, is smarmy enough to be useful."

"What does that mean?"

"He didn't tell you?"

"He didn't tell me we were a couple, either."

"That I can't confirm."

"You just wanted me to know that you knew?"

Selena nodded. "You catch on quickly."

"Not really. This time you are letting me know you do see me. I can't imagine that is by accident. Why?"

"I need you to watch Simeon for us."

"Why would I do that?"

"Because we have allowed the two of you to keep working and take over for Theory."

"Simeon is helping you?"

"I think he is helping himself; that's his thing. I would have thought you would know that about him by now."

"Yeah, it did occur to me. I still don't know why you need me, if you have him aptly motivated."

"Well, let's just say we don't trust in that completely."

"Clearly. And what is it you think I can do? And why do you think I would do it?"

"Unlike Simeon, I think you are a decent guy, Eli. Self-motivated, sure, but I have total confidence that you will keep your word to me."

"So why not come to me in the first place?"

"Honestly? Simeon could get us Theory; we didn't think you could. Simeon is cut from the same cloth, minus the addictions."

"You realize that Theory's girlfriend is your other?"

"Yeah, I know."

"That doesn't bother you?"

"A little, but despite the fact she looks like me, clearly we haven't the same taste, hence the 'alternate' in alternate universe."

"Must be interesting to have an idea of what another you could be like."

"Eh, not so much. Eli, more importantly, will you be our eyes on Simeon?"

"What's in it for me?"

"I will let you keep your place in the hierarchy here, and I won't arrest Simeon and toss him in a black site where he will never be seen or heard from again." [I deleted what seemed way too complicated.]

"What do I have to do for the privilege?"

"Just tell us what he is up to. He's smart; he will see us coming. We are hoping he doesn't see you."

Eli nodded. "You believe that he has no respect for me and therefore won't suspect me of spying for you?"

"I would say that covers it. Can we count on you?"

"We both get a pass no matter what he does?"

"Within reason, Eli. I can't provide a full get out of jail free card."

Eli pondered his choices, and when he realized he had virtually none, he capitulated.

"It's settled, then—use these to access the morgue. Tell Simeon they were here when you arrived," Selena said, handing Eli an envelope with key card and press passes.

She smiled at him, like a cat that got away with everything, and then left, swaying in the same sexy way that she came in.

CHAPTER 4

The morgue was relatively empty. It was late at night, which was when they thought the least attention could be drawn to their presence. It was a small crew, a single camera, with Theory mic'd with a wireless. Simeon and was there too, with one grip, and a PA. That was it.

They showed their press credentials at the gate, and again at the entrance to the private morgue.

"Let's get some exteriors of this place so we can say that it isn't the city morgue," Simeon suggested.

Simeon took the crew and guided them as they got their shots. Theory stepped out of the production van as the sound master wired him up.

"I can voice over the exteriors, yes?" Theory asked.

"Absolutely," Simeon chimed in.

"Fantastic. Let's get inside and do this in and out real fast. This place gives me the creeps. How the fuck did you get us access, anyway?"

"I'm just that good, which you know. I'm pretty sure you hired me because of my skill set."

Theory looked at him and nodded. "You know what we are going to see in there?"

"I have an idea, yes, and it isn't pretty, but it is fucking out of this world."

"Let's roll, then," Theory said, stiffening up.

"We don't get a lot of time, Theory, so I need you to understand what you are about to see."

"Dead people. I get it."

"No, you don't. Yes, they are dead people, but there are pairs of dead people, exact replicas of each other—one from this side, one from the alternative universe. The idea is they are somehow in such close proximity that they are affecting each other."

"That's good shit, Simeon, but how can we prove that?"

"Why do we have to? There are five pairs of identical dead people in there. That tells the story for you. People are dying in one universe, and their other is going down in the alternative. We have always suspected there were other universes, with other versions of us populating them, but we never perceived the notion that what happens in one could adversely affect the other. It's fucking momentous."

"I need a drink, and some shit."

"What you need is to do what you do, or we will not only lose this opportunity, but the show as well."

"What are you talking about?"

"Seriously, Theory, you haven't had a new show for almost four months! On top of that you are acting like a lunatic, running these crazy fucking experiments that are jeopardizing not only you, but your show, and all of us who have jobs there."

Theory was stunned, although obviously he shouldn't have been. He wanted a drink, he wanted a snort, he wanted Selena back. Theory wore all his addictions on his sleeve. He had been so caught up in finding Selena, and then avoiding the emotionality of his failure, drowning himself in booze and snorting enough coke to kill a small elephant, that he hadn't considered how many people's lives were connected to his success—or in this case, his failure. Then again, even without his laundry list of addictions to cater to, he probably still wouldn't give a shit.

"I know I'm a selfish prick, Simeon, but you realize that I am old, and that isn't likely to change."

"No shit? Fine, old man, get in there and give me some new footage that I can leak online and get people talking about you again."

Theory liked the idea of being talked about; feeding his ego was almost as high on the food chain as feeding his other needs.

"You are right, we need to get the show back up. It's been too long. Is the mic set?"

Simeon looked at the sound mixer, who was standing by like the rest of the skeleton crew, wondering if this segment was ever going to get made. She nodded at Simeon.

"Sound is good, Theory, so is picture; we are hot and biscuit here, daddy-o."

Theory cleared his throat and nodded. The cameraman stepped in front of him, the sound mixer got ready to record too.

"Good, then—roll picture, roll sound," Simeon ordered.

"Speed," the sound person said.

"I'm speeding too," echoed the cameraman.

Theory stood staring at the camera; the auxiliary light seemed to paralyze him like a deer. The few people all stared, waiting for the silence to break. It was excruciating.

"Theory, you should start," Simeon finally said.

He wasn't sure if he was out of practice, or just afraid he couldn't do it anymore. His hesitation proved neither, yet was evidence of both. Theory heard his producer talking to him, but that wasn't what snapped him out of it. It was her. The wisp of a thought that Selena would be back to him propelled his lips to start moving.

"We are outside a black site—a morgue, to be exact. We have exclusive access to something out of this world, literally. What you are about to see proves the impossible, that we are not alone, that we have exact replicas of ourselves in a universe so close to ours that lives are tethered to each other. If you die in one world, your counterpart dies too. The Black Syndicate doesn't want you to know that our worlds are crashing into each other, and no one knows what will happen. Let's go inside and have a look."

Theory made a dramatic turn, and the cameras followed him. Simeon skipped ahead, using the key cards that Selena gave Eli to gain access. The building was nondescript; anyone could have just passed it and hardly noticed it at all. It looked like a warehouse, where all things unwanted are kept. Hiding in plain sight, this place was right there, except for all the souped-up security.

Simeon led the way, accessing the ordinary door so they could record extraordinary things. Theory followed, and the cameras recorded what he saw as he saw it. At first there wasn't much to see—the hallways were bland and vague, giving away nothing of the nature of the place. Simeon wondered if Selena had fucked him to trap Theory. She had given Simeon exact instructions as to how to access the secret morgue, and when to do it as well. Selena had arranged for there to be a lapse in security and other personnel, but the window was short. Thankfully, Theory had not taken too much time to get his act together. For some reason, he had found motivation. Simeon wondered if somehow he thought he could get closer to his Selena, given what they knew. Simeon had little doubt that if someone told Theory he could cross over, he would, in the name of love. Simeon loved nothing and no one but himself, and therefore had zero respect for the pathetic state Theory had been living in, if one could call that living, but Simeon couldn't imagine feeling enough for someone that he would become murderous or self- destructive the way his mentor had. Then again, Simeon had little need for romance or other people in general. Sure, he had physical needs, sexual needs, but he equated sex with intimacy, even though on some level he knew that wasn't really what it was.

Simeon led the way, and Theory followed. "You sure we have this right, Simeon?"

"Yes. I've never been in here before; it all looks the same."

"You didn't vet the source? We could have a bunch of nothing here?"

"The source is gold, Theory."

"It better be."

"And if it isn't? Then what?" Simeon said turning to confront his boss.

Theory was a bit taken aback by his protégé's willingness to step up to him. Theory looked at him, locking eyes. The little prick seemed willing to go toe to toe. Theory was not. He was weakened by his vices and his confidence in himself had waned. Even when he was at the height of his success, he would never fight his own fight; he would have had someone else do it for him.

"Let's just hope you are right. You have any idea where the morgue is?"

"Not exactly, but it's here."

"Lead the way."

Simeon walked down the beyond-ordinary-looking hallway with doors on either side. He passed several of the doors, but Theory opened them, thinking his protégé must be missing something. Simeon missed nothing; the door he was looking for wouldn't be one that could simply be opened. It was one that would have to be accessed, and he had the key card to do it.

"This is it," Simeon said, standing at a replica of all the other doors, other than that this one was locked and had a high-tech scanner guarding it.

Theory struck a pose in front to the door. Simeon used the key card. It didn't work.

"Fuck."

Theory turned and looked at Simeon as he fumbled with the key card. "What's going on?"

"Not sure. I may not be doing it right."

Simeon tried again and again. It wasn't working. Theory and he both looked at the lock. "Let me try," Theory ordered.

"It won't work." Selena's voice stunned everyone, especially Theory.

The notorious host turned slowly. It was her, but not her. Despite the fact that they were identical, other than the white wisp, Theory could still tell the difference. Theory could feel his breath deepen. Even though it wasn't her, the sight of the copy of the woman he loved still affected him in a way he couldn't imagine.

Selena saw that her presence threw Theory, Simeon, and the crew. They all knew who she worked for, and the fear that came associated with the Black Syndicate. Theory wasn't afraid—he had seen a ghost—but Simeon was confused as to why she would be there.

Selena liked that she had this power over them, albeit all for different reasons, but she liked it. They weren't sure what she was up to, and neither was she.

"This will get you in." Selena swiped a key card and punched in a code. The door opened but no one moved.

"Go on, get your story."

"Why are you letting us in?" Theory asked

"Really, Elysium, I allow you everything. I thought you knew."

Selena turned and left. Everyone was relieved to see her go.

Theory scoffed but was glad that she was gone. Simeon and he shared a look; Simeon was so nervous that a bead of sweat dripped down his brow.

"Let's get in and out of here before they she changes her mind," Theory said.

"It's interesting, no?" Simeon asked.

"What is?"

"That your girlfriend's other is basically our worst nightmare."

"They both are something, that much I can say. How many times do you think a person can meet both personas? It's a rarity, I assure you."

"I hadn't thought of it like that, Theory. You are becoming profound again. It's actually nice to see you back."

"Oh, I doubt that. I'm not a complete moron, Simeon. I know you have designs on ascending the throne, as you should. I hired you because of your ambition, and I can't do this forever, or even recently. I want to find out how I can get my Selena back, and then all this is yours."

"Really?"

"Yup, you've earned it, you and Eli, but let's face it—he isn't the persona you are, or I am. Let him produce, give him some segments on air, but he will always be a better second fiddle."

"I appreciate the confidence, but let's do this before the Black Syndicate returns."

Theory nodded. Simeon pointed at the cameraman, who directed his equipment at Theory.

"Roll sound and picture."

"Rolling."

Theory was looking at the floor, and then like flipping a switch, he began talking to the camera. He was electric.

"We are about to find out what happens when worlds collide, together! Come on, follow me!"

Theory bounded into action. He hadn't been like this in a long time. Simeon was almost thrilled, but he couldn't have Theory be good again. That might cost him a job. Nah, the Blacks would take him down like they promised. At least Simeon hoped they would adhere to their end of the bargain. He was sure they would not, and that he would end up kept somewhere no one could find him. In an odd way, he wished to be hidden away from everything and everyone. Simeon had lied and cajoled his way into the life he was leading and had almost forgotten who he really was. He imagined that being kept somewhere he could somehow be safe from the world, and the world would be safe from him.

The room was filled with paired silver gurneys, that had paired dead people. They weren't exactly the same, yet they were. The only differences came from the environment each had lived in. One was so weathered, the other seemed polished by comparison. Exactly *not exact* were these people, or what was left of them.

The camera followed Theory as he looked in wonder at the unmatched matches. The host had seen a lot in his time, but this was something else entirely. The cameras rolled on him staring in wonder. It was as if he was putting on a show, but this reaction was genuine. This was real.

"This is incredible. In all my life, and all my experiences doing this show, I have never seen anything like this. Evidence of an alternative universe, where copies of us exist, but now it seems that the stakes are changing. People die there, their other dies here. Somehow, these separate universes are connected—are these worlds colliding?"

The camera panned over the sets of people, five in total, one just legs, but unmistakably belonging to the same person.

That was when it started.

First, not so noticeable, a breeze—was it a vent? No, it wasn't. Then isolated flashes of red lightning.

"Theory, this isn't right," Simeon said.

Theory looked at the bursts of light, "Film it," he instructed the cameraman.

Then a pounding noise.

"Theory! Fuck this, we need to go."

Simeon was scared, and the cameraman looked to him for an answer, but Theory stood pat, waiting, almost knowing something big was going to happen.

"Film that!" Theory instructed, pointing to the lightning.

The cameraman did, but he was shaking. Simeon made for the door.

"We need to get out of here!" Simeon grabbed his boss.

"We need to see what is happening!"

"Whatever it is, doesn't seem good. We can watch from a distance! Come on!"

Theory begrudgingly followed Simeon. The cameraman and sound mixer hustled out behind. In the hallway, there was more of the same: a preternatural wind, and red lightning at both ends of the hallway.

"Which way did we come from?" Simeon asked, disoriented.

"That way?" the camera guy pointed.

"No, we came in the other way," the sound mixer contradicted.

Then it happened. Out of the localized bursts it materialized. A massively muscular man, covered in a powder-blue dust and ruby-red tattoos with numbers and symbols was kneeling in the intensified lightning. It was alarming; the man who came from the lightning was kneeling, almost totally still, like a statue.

"Film that!" Theory yelled at his cameraman.

The man lifted the camera and pointed it at the muscular, tattoo-covered creature, but then at the opposite end of the hall more localized flashes produced what seemed to be another identical humanoid.

"Fuck!" Simeon screamed.

The first creature was moving now, obviously less disoriented from wherever he had materialized from. The other creature was starting to move as well. The four men were trapped in between the two creatures that seriously did not look friendly, compounded by the fact they rode in on a storm that was occurring indoors.

The creatures, however, didn't seem to register the men that were separating them; rather, they had arrived at the same point in time to fight each other. Once they got their bearings, they rushed at each other, not having a care that there were people in the middle of their arena.

The five men were trapped as the creatures made a beeline for each other. It was one of those moments like being on a plane when it has lost cabin pressure and is nose-diving into a deathly descent, when one knows one is going to die, yet is powerless to stop it, ceding control to whatever the power that fuels the universe, when one has no choice but to do so in the hopes that whatever comes next is painless.

The men seemed calm in the face of certain death. But death wasn't what came—not exactly. What came was a hole in the wall, a glowing one that spun like one of those child's toys made of foil and powered by wind or breath. Except this was a blue light, and out of it stepped *the other Theory*, black-haired and determined to save his alternate and his entourage.

Black-haired Theory reached out to his other and said, "Come with me if you want to live."

White Theory took his hand and was yanked into the spinning blue illumination evaporating into it. Simeon and the other men dove in after him as the Alpha and Omega crashed into each other just as the last man disappeared into the Light.

The creatures weren't after the men, and the tussle lasted only a short while. They tossed each other around briefly, but were so evenly matched that neither the Alpha or the Omega netted any advantage. They both stared at each other, the door to the morgue in between them. They didn't speak but appeared to understand that the fight was futile. Instead they converged at the door and both went in.

Once inside the morgue, both creatures took one of the pairs upon their shoulders, dividing them between them, as if they hadn't tussled at all minutes earlier. Now they were in sync. Each of them disappeared in a ball of light, much like the one Black Theory came from, and they departed with bodies slung over their massive shoulders.

Once they were gone, the room was still, and soon after they left, the other half of the pairs disappeared too. The room was entirely empty.

CHAPTER 5

The two Theorys stared at each other. Simeon and the crew, in turn, stared at the two versions of the same man.

"You saved me," White Theory said.

"As you saw in that morgue, I was highly motivated."

"Why is it happening?"

"The worlds are crashing into each other; when they were at a safe distance, this would never have happened."

White Theory looked around. The room was dark, but it also wasn't a room; it was as if they were outside, floating through the night sky. These men floated through space/time somehow, with universes all around them.

"Where are we?" he asked his counterpart.

"We are everywhere, but also nowhere."

"Real helpful, other Theory," Simeon quipped.

"If it wasn't for me, you wouldn't have been helped at all."

"Touché. What where those things back there?" Simeon asked.

"Ah, the big question."

"That's the big one?" Simeon quipped.

"Stop being an asshole, Simeon," White Theory instructed.

Black Theory chuckled. Then White Theory also chuckled. The crew looked at each other. It was eerie.

"Those creatures are protectors of space and time as we know it. When something gets fucked up, they fix it, and right now things are epically fucked."

"So, they weren't after us?" Simeon asked.

"I don't think so, but I can't say with certainty, either."

"What do you know for certain?" White Theory asked.

"Yeah, what good are you?" Simeon quipped.

White Theory looked at Black Theory. It was an odd exchange, as if they were talking without saying a word. The white-haired person began to laugh, almost uncontrollably.

"What the fuck is so funny, Theory?" Simeon asked, obviously annoyed.

"You don't get it, Simeon? This Theory started all this. It's his doing."

Simeon walked up to both men but stared at the black-haired version. "You are responsible for all the crap that has been fucking everything up? Crashing universes?"

"Me? Well, not exactly—he started it, actually," Black said, pointing to White.

"Him?"

"Me?"

"Yes, him; yes, you. Selena from my world—you remember falling for her?"

White Theory looked down.

"Yeah, well, that's how the whole mess started, by crossing over. When Selena made two of the same person in one universe, the Omega started to try to compensate by killing other Blacks, thinking they were the other to your Selena. I guess the fucker is glitchy, because clearly it knew there should only be one Selena, but it didn't quite identify her correctly; ergo the slew of dead assholes. The Alpha, him I wasn't aware of until the hallway, but it makes sense; there are multiple versions of everyone in every different dimension that exists."

"Selena crossing started this, that's what you are saying? But why would she do that? What was her reason?"

"She was sent by a man named Wu, because he felt that their universe was in jeopardy of being taken over by yours, and of course, he was right."

"Why would that be?" Simeon asked.

"You want to tell him? Or should I?" Black asked the White.

"How would I know?"

"Because we are the reason for all of this. We are different. While most have counterparts, we are more of a copy of each other."

"I am you, and you are me?"

"We are the same, whereas others have—well, others."

"If that is true, then how is it we are both here? Wouldn't there just be one of us?" White Theory asked.

"Yeah," Simeon seconded.

"Indeed," Black Theory agreed.

"You have been one and the same in both places the entire time?" Simeon asked.

Theory nodded. "Not one and the same, just the same."

"How?"

"What does it matter? You have survived; that's the important thing."

"OK, Theory, what the fuck do you want from me?" Simeon asked.

"Isn't that obvious? I want you to help me crash these universes."

"Why would you want to do that? And why would I help you?"

"You are an opportunist, that's why. I am the winning side, so logically, *that* is why you would help me do it. The reason behind it? To create a new world, where we can all be immortal. You want to be a god, don't you, Simeon?"

Simeon looked at White Theory, unable to answer, but feeling as if he had little choice but to see how this played out.

CHAPTER 6

Selena stood with Major Ott as a forensics team scoured the morgue. It had half the population that it had the last time Selena had been there.

"We are pulling the security footage now, but don't count on much. For some reason, when whatever happened here occurred, the cameras went out. It's nothing but static."

"Theory did this?" Ott asked.

"No. We do have the footage of the outside of the building. He never left."

"So, where is he?"

"I don't know, but the last we know he was here, and this."

Selena pulled up footage on a tablet, she showed Ott. The major looked at it in dismay, as he wasn't sure what he was seeing, other than Theory and his crew looking pinned and scared. Then the footage went into static.

"So, we have a missing lot of dead people and several missing assholes," Ott joked.

"Yes, sir, that would cover it."

"I take it we are looking at some level of quantum event."

Selena nodded. There was more to this, and Selena knew, but she could not quite put her finger on it.

"Where did the other bodies go? And where the hell is Theory?" Ott demanded.

The door to the morgue opened, and a Black Syndicate operative entered. He was one of Selena's. The man looked at her.

"What is it?" Selena asked.

"Perhaps you and the major might step out with me?"

Selena looked at Ott and nodded at her, and they followed the man into the hallway. Once the man had his superiors in private, he addressed them.

"We found someone who can possibly tell us what happened to Theory and his people, as well as the missing dead."

"Possibly?" Selena asked.

"I say that because his story is difficult to comprehend."

Ott looked at Selena, who in turn said, "Let's hear what he has to say."

The man nodded and gestured down the hall, and two the Black operatives escorted a security guard to Ott and Selena.

"Tell them what you told me,"

The guard was visibly shaken.

"What's your name?" Selena asked.

"Arnold," he responded meekly.

"Can you tell us what you saw, Arnold?"

Arnold was obviously shaken and scared.

"Guys, why don't you give us some space?" Selena asked the Black operatives.

The men nodded and moved away. Arnold was staring at his feet.

"It is important to know what you saw, no matter how unbelievable; that's our specialty."

Arnold looked up at Selena and nodded. "There were two of them."

"Two of who?" Ott asked.

"The guy from TV, the conspiracy guy with the white hair, but the other one had black hair, and the black-haired one pulled all of them into a light in the wall, then they disappeared, light and all. The blue naked men with all the red tattoos fought briefly before they disappeared into the walls, too. A few minutes later, they came out with three dead bodies apiece, and then they disappeared again."

Selena stared at Arnold and nodded.

"I had one drink, just one! I know I am not supposed to, but...."

"It's OK, Arnold. We believe you."

"You do?"

Selena nodded. "Absolutely. Thank you; that was very helpful. You can go."

Arnold waited a second, as if he didn't believe he could go, or that they believed him. He finally walked off, hoping they wouldn't scoop him up and take him away. He walked to the men who brought him in, and they ignored him as he walked by. A noticeable bead of sweat fell to the ground as he left the hall.

"What the fuck is he talking about?" Ott asked Selena.

"Theory's other saved him and his crew, probably in a self-preservation kind of way."

"You think the other Theory knows if you die in one world, you die in another?"

"No way to be sure, but why else would he show up to save his doppelgänger?"

"And these blue assholes with the tags?"

"That one is new to me, sir. They took the people from the other side; maybe they are course correctors of some kind?"

Ott nodded. "That would make sense. But the guard seemed to think they were after Theory."

"Perhaps it just appeared that way, incidental. He is a civilian."

"If Theory can cross over, then so can we," Ott pointed out.

"He had help."

"So? Why can't we? This asshole seems to be at the epicenter of whatever is going on. Who knows what consequences we will incur? Figure it out."

"Yes, sir."

Selena watched as Ott walked away. She wondered how she could possibly solve this mystery.

CHAPTER 7

Eli sat in the office, nervous. Simeon was now four hours late coming back to the production office, and he couldn't be reached. Neither could Theory or the two crew that had been dispatched to the site Selena had given them access to.

Eli called the crew guys—straight to voicemail. He tried Theory; it was the same. He didn't try Simeon, not yet—Eli didn't want to seem needy, although he was feeling needy, very much so. He rationalized he could call, given the circumstances. It *was* an emergency. Eli paced. Simeon didn't tell him what it was they were chasing, but it was exciting, and Theory was back. He wasn't chasing *her*.

Eli called Theory's cell. Voicemail. He left a message. He felt paralyzed and utterly alone. He always felt alone, but now even more exponentially. He had avoided human connection for the most part, and this was the reason why. People just let other people down. It was a fact of the human condition.

"He's gone. He won't get your message where he is."

Simeon turned to see Selena, Theory's Selena.

"Where is he?"

"There is a war going on. Simeon and Theory, both of them are in the middle of it. If I am right, he crossed over somehow. It's just a gut feeling, but I have a sense for these things."

"You realize that asshole was chucking people off that building to find a way to get you back?"

145

"Yeah. We saw the aftermath on the other side."

"Why are you back? Why didn't you just stay there?"

"I never wanted to leave. If you had been there, you would believe me."

"You got that right."

"I came back for him."

"Sure you did."

"The man who sent me here did that so that I could spy on your Theory, as his other is creating the havoc that is affecting both worlds. I was then sent back to kill your Theory, so that the one from our side will also die."

"Yeah? Why don't you just kill that one?"

"It's not so simple; our Theory has unique abilities. He is elusive. But if he dies, yours would too, and I can't have that."

"What do you want, Selena?"

"I need your help."

"What good am I to you?"

"You have more value than you know, Eli, but what good you are, is to help me save this universe, and hopefully Theory in the process."

"What about your home? You don't want to save it, too?"

Selena bowed her head. "I am not proud of where I have come from, it is the most miserable place I've ever been. They have asked me to assassinate the man I love in a vain effort to save what is already dead. I don't care if that world survives. In fact, when I think of it, I would prefer that it didn't."

"What's in it for me?"

"Same as always Eli—survival. Perhaps even you might enjoy some advancement."

Eli looked at Selena, and as he did, he wondered if her other were equally or more manipulative.

"Fuck it, sure. What do I have to lose?"

"Exactly!" Selena said, pleased.

"So now what?"

"We need to find my other."

"Great. You know who she is here, right?"

"That's why we need her help."

Eli shook his head. He couldn't believe he was involving himself in this, but what else could he do?

CHAPTER 8

Wu looked at his adjunct. He had been captured in the compound that was holding the 5-Gen together. More and more of the substance had been deployed and more prisoners and guards alike had to be frozen in time and space so that the patch of torn universe could hold. Soon, the entire 5-Gen would be drowned in the synthetic compound, and all of the inhabitants frozen in it waiting to be free of it all, and that would happen in the form of the place being crushed.

The Captain was up against it, and he had no discernible solution. He had his scientists working on a way to create a stable way to transverse worlds. Selena had survived being tossed off a high cliff and a building in the alternate world, but Wu himself wasn't willing to take that chance. He rationalized that he was too important. Perhaps if he could speak to his counterpart over there, they could figure out a way to co-exist again.

Selena hadn't reported meeting Wu's other. He wondered if she had, but chose not to tell him because the other was worth so little to his universe. Wu, of course, found that hard to accept, but it was possible. If she was holding back, to spare him certain embarrassment, he was grateful. Wu would hate it if he had no meaning or purpose, even if it were him but not him.

Wu looked around. The 5-Gen was even more desolate than normal. He had locked down the prisoners; they weren't even let out for work detail. It would be this way indefinitely—it had to be. Wu didn't care if any of the prisoners died or remained in stasis, but he did care about his men; the less movement, the less likely a guard would get sucked into a tear in the universe or be trapped in the compound as a result.

Still, he had to do something. The 5-Gen was being torn apart, and he didn't know how much more time they had before the next rip in the fabric of his universe was the last one. Wu moved carefully to the labs, being ever aware that at any moment he could fall victim to a tear in his world.

Inside the labs, there were compound-filled corners, too. No space in the 5-Gen had been immune to degeneration. The scientists moved around with purpose, clearly understanding the sensitive nature of what was happening, and that time was of the essence.

Wu stood in the room expecting to be recognized and reported to, but men in white lab coats ran around the room or stood at stations staring at things. Wu did not understand what the men were doing and less so why they would ignore him at such a critical time. Finally, out of frustration, Wu unholstered his service weapon and shot two times in the air. The men of science stopped in their tracks, and all turned to look at the Captain.

"What is happening?" Wu asked the stunned men.

One of the scientists came up to the Captain. He was sweating profusely. "I am sorry, Captain, but we have a development,"

"What is it?"

"Sir, it would be easier to show you. Besides, I have no explanation."

Wu nodded nervously. He followed the man in the lab coat to an area encased in the orange, translucent compound. There were people trapped inside it, which wasn't out of the ordinary, but who or what was encased with it was the odd part. The Captain squinted his eyes as if he couldn't quite believe what he was seeing.

"I don't understand," the Captain said.

"I can't say we do either."

"What can you say? You must know something!" Wu responded.

"They appeared in here, when before they were not. Which as you know is impossible, unless they have the ability to travel between worlds."

Wu looked inside at the pair of nude blue men covered in red tattoos. Both men, if you could call them that, were carrying someone. The one with the Omega on his back carried half a man, legs only. The other creature had a full person.

"I recognize the woman—she is a prisoner!"

"That is correct, Captain. She is one of many who disappeared without a trace. Our speculation is that her other died and somehow, she joined her on the other side, also dead. We further speculate that these creatures are somehow trying to course-correct the universes crashing into each other. We assume that the legs belong to someone we know, too."

"These things can fix whatever is happening?"

"I have no way have knowing that, Captain; it is merely a guess."

"Can you get one or both of them out of the patch?" Wu asked.

"If you order it, we can try."

Wu nodded. "I order it."

"Thank you, sir!"

And with that, the men of science of the 5-Gen huddled together and left Wu standing staring at creatures he didn't understand, wondering what he had just authorized.

CHAPTER 9

Simeon watched as the two identical men spoke in an animated manner to each other. He couldn't hear their conversation, but it was obviously intense. Whatever the nature of the conversation, it was enthusiastic, to be sure, and they obviously agreed to something. It was about the only comradeship in the room. Simeon was wondering where they were and how to get home, or if they could get there. The two crew guys were bickering over something.

The two Theorys laughed, but it was the white-haired version's last one, as black-haired embraced him in a bizarre way, and as it turned out, the hug wasn't just a hug. The two men became one. They merged, and as they became one man, the only way one would know that they were one man, but really two, was the hair—half white and half black, but one Theory.

"What the fuck?" Simeon said.

The crew guys and Simeon all approached Theory 3.0. The three men stared at him, as he took stock of his new self.

"Theory! What just happened?" Simeon asked.

Theory looked up and smiled. "The inevitable!"

"You wanna elaborate? Or should I be grateful that you turned two assholes into one?"

"We have always been one, Simeon."

"Say what now?"

"We weren't ever two separate people. No one is, really."

"You are both total ass hats. Or you are one massive ass hat, now. This was the plan? Fucking calculated? For what?"

"World-building!"

"The two worlds are colliding—you are destroying, not creating."

"Yes! That is 100% correct! Bravo, Simeon. I always liked you! I mean I hated you because you are a pedantic, overly ambitious fucker, but I like it! You remind me of me."

"You are crushing universes, and you believe we are on par?"

"Crushing? Well, yes, I suppose that is true, but only to create a new place."

"You are willing to potentially destroy two universes to create your own?"

"No! Not potentially—actually destroy! And it's worth it! Those invited in to my universe will be GODS!"

Simeon looked at Theory with disdain. Theory sensed this disapproval and he moved to an empty space in the room. He moved to the crew guys. "You guys must be hungry. Can I offer you some fruit? "

The cameraman nodded excitedly. "I am starving!"

"You are Ben, right?" Theory asked

"That's right, yes."

"I am going to get you that fruit, Ben right now, if you are willing to volunteer for a tiny experiment. It will be quick. I promise."

"Sure, whatever you want."

Simeon was getting nervous. It felt like a deal with the devil.

"Great!"

And with a wave of his hand, Theory produced a glass table with a glass bowl with five perfect persimmons in it. A sharp knife on the table lay untouched by Ben as he grabbed a fruit. It crunched as he bit into the flesh. Theory turned to look at Simeon and winked.

The sound man took a persimmon as well, and also bit into one with ecstasy.

"Good, right? It's ambrosia, fruit of the gods," Theory said.

Simeon watched as Theory picked up the knife. "Theory...."

Theory looked at Simeon and gave a wink and a smile right before slashing the shocked Ben's throat. It was cut deeply, and it opened and bled. Poor Ben gasped and grabbed at what should have been a fatal strike, yet aside from having lost his ability to speak, he did not die nor even fall from what should have been a fatal blow.

"What the fuck, Theory?" Simeon protested.

The sound mixer wondered if he was next and backed up cautiously.

"What, Simeon? I am merely giving you a preview as to our new universe. GODS! We are immortal, you are immortal!"

"What, are you going to slit my throat to prove it? Fuck you, Theory!"

"Fuck me? I did you and these others a favor. Did you not hear me? We can't die!"

"Yeah, well—right now the idea of spending an eternity with you in this place isn't exactly a plus," Simeon said, gesturing to the small space they shared.

"This is just the seed of the great plan my friend. We will all have loads of space and time to create whatever we want. Once the other two worlds are gone we will have so much space to be and do whatever we want. We just need to get a few people, like Noah's ark, they meld with their others and then voila! We have infinite time and space to create a new paradise!"

"Wow, Theory, that's fucking nuts," Simeon said, shaking his head.

"Is it? I am trying to make a better existence, Simeon! You don't see that?"

"I see this," Simeon said, pointing to Ben trying to make sense of his cut throat.

"You don't have to," Theory said, frowning.

Theory moved to Ben and pushed him, and as he did, the man disappeared. The sound mixer was backing up slowly—not that this bizarre pocket of space and time had much room in it. The "seed," as Theory had put it, had yet to grow.

"Where did he go?"

"A place where that injury will hurt a lot more than a lost voice," Theory said before turning to the sound mixer. "Sorry, you gotta go too."

The man backed up into nothingness, as he disappeared too. Simeon looked at Theory. "I am not afraid of you or of dying!"

"I know! Besides, you still work for me!"

"So did they!"

"True, Simeon, true. But you have value. I know you don't see it now, but you will. Now, you want to meet your other? Meld up?"

"Why the fuck would I want to do that?"

"To feel complete, Simeon. These worlds were never meant to be split. You have been living as a half a person your entire life. I can make you whole again. Give me a minute."

Theory walked forward, disappearing as he did. Simeon was antsy. He couldn't imagine what would come next. Simeon paced around the room. He looked out the window; it was as if wherever the "seed" of Theory's universe was in the midst of the cosmos. It was ethereal—stars and nebulas floated by. It was scary and beautiful. Scary beautiful.

Theory came walking out of nothingness, and he wasn't alone. With him was a bent-over man, wearing what appeared to be a tawdry canvas grey matching pants and shirt. The man looked as if he had come from living in a bowl of dust. He was gaunt and dirty.

Simeon shivered at the sight of his other; even though he couldn't see his face, he knew who it was. It is an odd moment to be sure, when you come to meet a you…that's not you.

"So, you can meld with him if you like, and become whole, cosmically speaking."

Simeon looked at his doppelgänger. It was a disturbing sight, to be sure. "No thanks, Theory; I really don't want to be like you."

Theory looked at Simeon with curiosity. "Why wouldn't you? I cannot die."

"I really hope there is no truth to that."

"Meld with him and feel the power I do!"

"Not interested."

Theory's eyes narrowed. "You are being a fool."

"You can return me to my correct time and space?" Simeon asked.

"Of course I can, but why would you want that?"

"Because I can't stand being around you. I assume now that you are all connected with yourselves, I can now take your place and run the show, which is why I was working for you in the first place."

Theory stared, his eyes boring into the soul of Simeon. His other tried to sneak a peek as to what was happening, but probably understood from the tenor of the conversation that it was anything but pleasant.

"So that's how you want it, Simeon?"

"That's how I want it."

Theory nodded and suddenly moved to Simeon's other, the poor creature unaware, as Theory plunged his whole hand into the man's chest as he pushed him backwards with his other hand. The man disappeared as if he never had been there, though his still-beating heart in Theory's clenched fist was proof that he had been.

"Fuck!" Simeon said, backing away.

"Fuck indeed. He is dead back in the hell he came from, and if you go back to your universe, you will die as soon as you materialize in it. Your only means of survival is to stay here."

Simeon stared at his keeper in disbelief. Although he wanted to tell himself it wasn't true, he knew it was. He really had no choice but to submit to Theory's capriciousness yet again; it appeared to be his lot in life, regardless of universe.

CHAPTER 10

Eli couldn't believe he was going straight into the mouth of the enemy. Selena insisted that they needed to see Selena Black. Eli hated both Selenas. They both seemed nice enough, except for the fact that regardless of what world they came from, they clearly both had agendas other than what they disclosed at the outset.

Between the company and destination, Eli was worried about Simeon. He texted him almost every hour, acting more like a husband nervous that his significant other couldn't be found. Of course, Eli was just a one-time lover, but he thought they had really connected. That, and Eli always equated sex with love—a fatal flaw, to be sure, but he couldn't help that.

Eli had not only not been loved, but abused—physically, by his alcoholic father, and sexually by two of his teachers. Being poor made him an easy victim on both fronts, but he didn't complain. The sexual abuse actually soothed the abuse at the hands of his father, but both things fucked him up royally, and now Simeon, whom he had trusted with the gift of his sexuality, the only form of love he could safely give, was MIA.

Eli knew it wasn't only Simeon that was missing. The two crew guys and Theory also had seemingly fallen off the planet. Eli was still a wreck, both because of his missing lover, but also because he was in a car with his boss' otherworldly girlfriend, who was too anxious to meet her doppelgänger.

"This is a bad idea," Simeon said.

"Maybe," Selena said, looking at Eli sitting in the passenger's seat, sweating nervously.

"Maybe? That's why you have us out here? Your other is a bad woman. I mean, I know she is you, but it doesn't mean she is you."

"I am aware of that, but she is also in a unique position to help us. Believe me, if I weren't desperate, I wouldn't be doing this."

"I don't know what you think you know, but the organization she works for is highly secretive. They operate strictly out of black sites, and unless she wants to be found, we won't be able to locate her."

"That's why we have to get her to come to us."

Eli looked at Selena as she drove outside the city and toward the more rural areas. The whole time he had been under the impression that she knew where she was going, but now he was not so sure. Finally, they stopped. Selena pulled over to the side of the road. She took a deep breath.

"This is where you think Selena Black is coming? To a field, in the middle of nowhere?"

"Yup," she said, getting out of the car.

Eli got out too. He stood and watched as Selena walked into the golden field. He shook his head. "Christ," he muttered to himself and then followed her. "Why would she do that?"

"Can you shut up a minute?" Selena snapped.

Eli stopped in his tracks. He wondered why he agreed to come; then he thought of Simeon. He did shut up—what else was he going to do at this point? He took a deep breath and followed Selena.

She stopped in a clearing. Selena briefly looked about and then reached into her bag and pulled out a handheld device that wasn't familiar to Eli. He wanted to ask what it was but decided to respect her request to be silent.

Selena walked around with the device. Was she checking for something? Taking a measurement?

"Here!"

Eli looked at the nothingness of the area, wondering what the excitement was all about. Selena then found a rock and used it to start digging. Finally, she looked up. "You going to just stand there? Help me dig."

Eli grabbed a rock, and the pair loosened the earth. Once they had a shallow hole, Selena tossed her rock away, and said, "That is enough."

Eli wiped the sweat from his forehead and tossed his rock. He stood as Selena flicked a switch on the device and then hurried it into the shallow hole. She stood up and dusted herself off. She caught Eli looking at her.

"What just happened?" Eli asked.

"In this place, the space between universes is particularly thin, and obviously remote. This is a perfect place to build a bridge."

"A bridge?"

"We are hoping that we can create a safe way to pass between worlds. The methods we have employed so far have not exactly been safe or desirable. But if we don't work together, both universes could face collapse. This device was designed by 5-Gen scientists to stabilize a portal. After that, they can come here and work with the other Selena's organization, and hopefully together we can stop what is happening."

"All that from the thing you buried?"

"All that, hopefully, yes, her organization will undoubtedly pick up the disturbance that this device will create, she will come, and we will meet her and hopefully she will agree with our ideas."

Eli shook his head. "You really have no idea who you are over here, do you?"

"We will see."

CHAPTER 11

Wu stood nervously watching as his scientists experimented with a laser designed to penetrate the compound that was holding the universe together. He stared at the creatures that looked like men but were clearly much, much more than that. They appeared to have a blue skin and were covered in red tattoos. Wu wondered if they could save the 5-Gen. If they couldn't figure out how to end the crashing of the universes, what would happen to them, and the populations of both worlds?

"How long?" Wu asked no one in particular, but also everyone.

The science team was concentrating so diligently on the laser that they didn't hear Wu.

"HOW LONG?"

That got their attention. A man in a lab coat approached the Captain.

"Captain Wu, this is an unknown process to us. It could take five minutes; it could take five months."

Wu grabbed the man by his white coat, scaring the scientist senseless. "We don't have five months!"

The Captain was choking the man so intensely that he couldn't breathe. The other scientists were afraid of Wu, and therefore didn't intervene. Fear is a lonely place in the hearts of men. No one wanted to help their comrade for fear of what might happen to them.

Wu must have felt the eyes of the room on him, and finally he let go of the man, who backed away as he caught his breath.

"Someone get me when you have succeeded!" Wu said before practically goose-stepping out of the medical facility.

The men of science got back to unearthing the unknown, as if nothing had happened.

Wu moved through the grey yard, looking at all the compound that peppered the prison. There was more and more compound--he didn't need the men of science to tell him the situation was worsening. Wu marched to his office. He entered to see a strange man sitting at his desk with his feet up on it.

"Who are you!" Wu demanded.

"Captain Wu, I presume?"

Wu looked at the man, curious why he wasn't scared of him.

"I am Wu."

"Fantastic! I am here at the behest of a mutual friend. Elysium Theory?"

"He is not a friend; he is a tormentor."

"Shit, brother, that asshole torments everyone!"

"I can have my men in here and take you prisoner!" Wu blurted.

"Yeah, that's just not going to happen."

"We can see."

"Well, you can do that, but it would only be an embarrassment for you."

"And why would that be?" Wu asked.

"Because I am here, but I am not here."

Wu looked at the man sitting in his chair—he was there, unless his eyes deceived him or he had lost his mind. But then the man got up and walked to Wu, and then through Wu. The Captain turned—this was the next person to haunt him?

"Who are you, and what do you want?"

"That's the question I have been waiting for. My name is Simeon White, and I work for the asshole who is destroying all this," Simeon said, waving his hand around the room.

"Theory."

"Yes, Theory. He is destroying your world, and the universe you sent your agent to."

"Why? Why is he doing that?"

"He needs the space to create a new plane of existence—one where we can be gods. Theory wants you to join him there, leave this hell behind."

Wu chuckled. "I don't believe that at all. He has been tormenting me for a long, long time. Disrupting operations at the 5-Gen, pulling it apart."

"Yes, I believe that may have been his way of saying that he likes you. It is an odd way, to be sure. You should see how he decided to keep me around."

Wu looked at the specter of Simeon. "And if I say no?"

"I guess you go down with the ship. Your world is collapsing, and fast. When it ceases to exist, so will you."

Wu nodded. "And if I agree, how would that work?"

"I am really glad you asked that," Simeon said.

"So am I."

Wu whipped around to see Theory. His hair was no longer all black, but half white as well. He looked like a lunatic.

"You!" Wu exclaimed

"In the flesh! Well, actually astral projections, but whatever." Theory nodded at Simeon.

"My work is done here, Captain. It's a real shit hole you are running here; of all the hells in all the universes, I am pretty sure yours is the worst."

Theory laughed at his protégé's sass. He couldn't have said it better himself. "There is a surprise for you when you return. Good job today. We will join you shortly."

Simeon nodded and then disappeared into the nothingness from which he came.

"You could do that too, Wu. It all can be yours…."

"At what price?"

"Indeed, that is true. But it is nothing that wouldn't be paid anyway."

"You have been driving me mad for a long time, Theory."

"I am aware, Captain. You even sent my girlfriend back to try and kill me. You didn't count on her catching feelings. Women love bad boys."

"What do you want?"

"I want you to cede the 5-Gen for collapse. In exchange, you survive and become immortal, too, in my new universe."

"Everyone here would die?"

"Is that a problem? I would have thought it might have been a perk."

Wu considered whether he was correct—no pressure to not fuck up what his father and grandfather had built before him, no more of the stress that came with the destruction that was happening now. Granted, all this was at the hands of his nemesis, but that would change if their agendas aligned.

"I have a son and a wife."

"You also have a collapsing universe. It will get to that eventually with or without you, Wu. It is just a matter of when, and whether you survive it. If you are willing to sacrifice the ship that is going down anyway...I am prattling on. What do you think?"

Wu bowed his head. "Give me some time to think and get my affairs in order."

Theory nodded. "Twenty-four hours, Wu, understood?"

"Understood."

Wu sat down, and when he looked up, his nemesis was gone. A man needed to know when he was beaten, and despite the fact that it looked like he was, his instinct told him he shouldn't give in.

He sat at his desk briefly and then remembered that he had a small bottle of liquor in his drawer. He rarely drank, but this was a good as of time as any. He poured a drink of the brown liquid and drank it with certain desperation. He repeated the procedure. His body filled with warmth. The numbness felt delicious. He looked at the bottle, wondering if there was enough of it to kill him and absolve him of any or all responsibility.

Wu decided not to give in to more temptation. He had to see if there were other options. The only solution would have to come from where the most resources were directed; the science. He took one last swig of liquor and placed the bottle back into his desk drawer.

Wu marched out into the empty yard. It was somehow more grey than usual. It was odd to have no one else out there, but also less dangerous for prisoners and guards alike. It was then Wu realized that if he were to be caught in a tear in the universe, no one would know until he was nowhere to be found. He quickened his pace to the labs.

When he got there, all the men were gathered around the compound, leaning in to observe as closely as possible. Wu was buzzed enough not to demand the attention of his science team. Instead, he moved as close to the circle as he could.

"What have you discovered?"

"Ah! Captain! This is very interesting. Look closely at the images on the creatures. You see the clocks?"

Wu moved in closer and nodded.

"We believe they correct time and space from anomalies. It has us theorizing that we can reset time and avoid the destruction that appears imminent."

"Reset time? How?"

"We think we can get one of these creatures to do it for us, by sending them to wherever the person responsible is and detonating an implosive device."

"Implosive? You mean explosive?"

"No, sir, I mean implosive. We detonate it within the confines of his space/time and it will be sucked into the device, in theory destroying everything in it forever and resetting the timelines in the two other worlds we know of. The challenge would be freeing one of these guys and convincing him to do it."

"You don't have to convince them of anything."

"Sir?"

"I was invited to the madman's world. I bought some time to see if there was a way out of this, and thanks to you guys, there is."

"Captain, I am not sure you are understanding. If you travel to wherever he is and set the implosion, you will likely not survive."

"Maybe I will—you said time is reset, no? Wouldn't we go back to how things were before all this started?"

The man in the lab coat considered. "Yes, I suppose it is possible, but in all likelihood, it is a suicide mission."

"I understand, but we have little choice and one opportunity. How long to prepare the implosion?"

"We can have you fitted within the hour."

"Good, make it happen. I will be in my office until then."

And with that Wu walked off, now scared but proud that he could save things, and if he were lucky, save himself too.

CHAPTER 12

Simeon stood looking at the stars in the window as they went by. It was both awe-inspiring and the loneliest place in all the worlds. He wondered what would happen. He wondered what he wanted to happen. He hated Theory, regardless of the space and time from which he originated; then again, he also hated himself for getting himself in this position.

Simeon thought of Eli. He didn't want to miss him, but he did. He had never had a romantic relationship with anyone, man or woman. Simeon had equated sex with love and affection. That was the extent to he was willing to allow intimacy, but now he craved it, needed it. It was one of those lonely moments we all know where we stare out a window and long not to be alone, to be with someone who wants to be with us, that longing for human connection that can elude all of us.

"That was well done, Simeon. I am proud of you."

Simeon didn't turn to see Theory. He knew his voice and wanted to linger in his imaginings of being with Eli just a little bit longer.

"I have something for you, as a reward," Theory said.

Simeon sighed. Whatever it was, he was sure he didn't want it, but he turned around anyway. And there he was, Theory, standing there and in his arms, he held the other Simeon, ragged and looking at least mostly dead.

"You are gifting me a dead version of me? How thoughtful. Really, you shouldn't have."

"You can meld with him and be whole, and of course you can move about, not being stuck here, if you so choose. That is my gift to you."

Simeon walked up to the him that was not him. He was dirty and too thin. "Will this help him at all?"

"Of course it will; you will be whole. It is a position of strength that no one besides me has ever enjoyed, but that will change as we create my utopia. Join me, and with him."

Simeon didn't know what to believe. Theory had clearly manipulated the situation. This was what he wanted, the melding, but he had also framed it as the way to *not* be stuck in the 'utopia,' so what choice did he have? All he had to go on was what this asshole he had somehow aligned himself with had told him, and this asshole was playing God—how could he trust him? What choice did he have?

Theory placed the other Simeon on a white table.

"Is he dead?" Simeon asked.

"We are all dead to some degree, especially where he came from."

Simeon looked at his alternate self. They were hardly mirror images; it was as if all the ugly on Simeon's inside was showing on the other Simeon's outside.

"What is that place? Hell on Earth?"

Theory looked at Simeon and deadpanned, "Something like that. I have to go collect something from there—a gift, really, for you."

"Now you are gifting things to me?"

"You will get it when I get back. You want to join with him? Become whole?"

"Seems to be all the rage."

"It is. You will feel complete for the first time. It is an unparalleled experience."

Simeon wasn't convinced, but he knew he would have to comply if for no other reason than to buy some time to figure a way out and to garner some more confidence.

"It doesn't matter that he is dead?"

"We can change that," Theory answered.

Megalomania is a scary thing to watch. The Theory Simeon knew was obsessive, but it seemed when he melded with his other self, the pathology of his ego increased exponentially. Simeon knew he had to comply with what Theory was asking if he were to have a chance of escape, yet at the same time he wondered what he would become if he did.

"Your power seems limitless, Theory."

This statement seemed to please him. "Soon, that will be true. Now, if you will excuse me."

"Sure."

Theory looked at Simeon and his other on the slab, and then turned and walked away, disappearing as he did. Simeon was relived to be alone, until he realized that he was with some shadow of himself.

Simeon wondered why Theory had left him to think about his counterpart on the slab, but he knew it was likely done on purpose. This new Theory was more calculating than the one he had known. He wondered how he might change too. This other version of him seemed weak and useless, other than not being stuck in this nascent universe, he didn't know what good it would do him.

Simeon touched the face of his other. His skin was dry, and he opened his eyes. Simeon had thought he was dead, he lay so still. The poor creature was weak. He barely kept his eyes open. At least he was alive.

"You hungry?" Simeon asked him.

The gaunt counterpart managed a nod. Coming back from the dead can make one ravenous, Simeon thought to himself. There was fruit, that Theory had called ambrosia. Fucking Theory and his God complex had really gotten away from him.

Simeon sliced the persimmon and fed his other. Poor thing could barely swallow.

"You know who I am?" Simeon asked.

He shook his head no.

"I am you, but not you."

He looked perplexed.

"Don't worry; soon you will be us."

"Glad to hear it!" Theory had returned.

Simeon turned to see his host. He carried with him another body. It was Eli's other.

"I thought a utopia for you would include your boyfriend."

"How considerate. How did you know?"

"Omniscience is a bonus of the new me—try it on for yourself."

"He seems weak. Will it affect me?"

"Yes, you will be more powerful than you can possibly imagine."

"What do I do?"

"Just lie back and enjoy the ride."

Then Theory made two Simeons into one super Simeon. He was right; somehow the newly formed being felt whole, when before he now realized he did not. Filled with energy, Simeon believed in that moment he could take on the world, and then he realized that if he could get Eli to meld, there would be two of them against one Theory—maybe there was a way out of this.

CHAPTER 13

"We should get back. I have no idea how strong this is. I mean my guess is very strong, if it can blow a hole in between universes."

Eli shook his head as he backed up. Desperate times, he supposed. They cleared the area and went back to the vehicle. They had almost made it back to the car when the charge went off. It sent a vibration so strong that it knocked both Selena and Eli down. The windows of the car shattered.

"Jesus," Eli said.

"We should look. If we succeeded, they will detect the tear, and who knows how they will arrive? I would assume by air."

"I'm telling you, you will regret this."

"No, Eli, I won't. We have no choice. I don't like it any better than you do, but if we don't get my counterpart out here, we will have no way of making the bridge work."

"Even if you get her out here, you realize there is no guarantee that she will agree with your plan."

"Leave that to me."

They made their way back to the site. It had worked. There was a shimmer in the fabric of the universe, a wound in the flesh of the cosmos. It was as if a fun house mirror had been installed in the clearing in the field, except in lieu of a distorted image, there was only distortion. Where there should be a field, there was what could only be described as gray on the other side. Whatever was over there was almost a black and white world compared to the Technicolor one they were in.

Eli was drawn toward the strangeness. He moved toward the shimmer, fascinated by what might lie on the other side.

"Don't get too close," Selena advised.

"This is where you're from? There is so little there."

"There is more than you can see."

"Uh-huh. I am sure. Listen, how long are we going to stand around here? Theory and Simeon have been MIA since going to report on some Black site, and now you want to attract those same assholes who probably disappeared them?"

"Look, we haven't any choice. I know you can't wrap your head around this, but we are about to incur an extinction event from both sides. We don't have the luxury of trying to figure another way out of this. It's all hands on deck, even if some of those hands belong to probable enemies."

The sounds of the helicopters caused both Selena and Eli to look skyward.

"My money is on us being fucked, and not in the fun sense," Eli said pessimistically.

Selena looked at him, wondering if he might be correct, but knowing she had to roll the dice.

The two black choppers touched down, each carried men with weapons and tactical gear. Four men per chopper all came at Selena and Eli, pointing weapons at them. The pair raised their hands, and as they did, the other Selena emerged from one of the helicopters. Her hair was back in a slick ponytail and she was dressed as she always was, in a skin-tight black lycra ensemble.

The choppers shut off, and Selena strangely went right up to her other instead of looking at the hole in the universe. The only way to differentiate the two was the hair—one was up and the other was down. Theory's Selena of course had the wisp of white too.

Selena Black came face to face with Selena White. They stood staring, as if speaking somehow, yet not moving their lips. It seemed to be a standoff of some sort.

"You did this? Why?" Black asked.

"I am sure you understand the reason."

The staring resumed.

"What have you done with him?" Eli blurted out.

"What have I done with whom?" Black asked.

"Simeon. And Theory!"

"Last I saw them, they were alive and well. They didn't materialize on a TV segment? I assumed they were back on air instead of tossing innocent assholes off buildings."

"I am afraid that was my fault," White chimed in.

"Your fault?"

"It was the only way to transverse worlds—well, at least for our side. Until now."

"This is why you did this? We can all just cross over whenever we want without having to reach terminal velocity?" Black asked.

"No, this is leadership so both sides can figure out how to stop the worlds from crushing each other."

"I see," Selena Black said, nodding. "Thing is, our universe isn't collapsing. I am pretty sure that aside from your little stunt here, the problem is on your end."

Selena White sighed. "Yet you came out here, in the middle of nowhere in a helicopter, because you aren't concerned about it?"

Selena Black managed a brief smile. "What do you want from me?"

"Cooperation. Just come talk to the people on the other side. Share information—let's figure out how to stop this."

"And you want me to go over there with you to achieve that?" Black asked.

"If you are authorized to negotiate, then yes."

"You want me to just enter that world without vetting you or the situation, merely because you said it's an emergency?" Black probed.

"I think you know your world is jeopardy, Selena. I think you have tears here too; maybe not as bad as the ones in the 5-Gen, but still, the longer we wait, the less likely we will be able to come up with a prompt solution."

The two Selenas resumed their standoff. Eli looked at the assholes in the tactical gear standing around as if it meant something. All Eli could think was—how could it have meaning? He was fairly sure that extinction event was a sure thing.

"You two going to do something here? Or is it going to be one big staring contest?" Eli asked finally.

They both looked at him simultaneously. It made Eli shiver.

"I don't trust you or this," Black said, pointing toward the funhouse-mirror-like crack between worlds.

"Fine!" Eli said

He marched into the mirror and disappeared into it.

CHAPTER 14

Simeon felt better than he ever had before. His mind worked at break-neck speed, and all his senses were heightened. He watched his hand as he waved it through the air. It was as if as if he could feel the molecules in between his fingers.

Theory watched as his protégé adjusted to his new, whole self. A smile crept across his face.

"Now you understand why I wanted this for you?"

"One hundred percent, yes I do."

"Good. Now we are going to pay the Captain another visit."

"I like the projection. I can't imagine what it will feel like whole."

"That will have to wait," Theory confessed. "This time we go in the flesh."

"Why?"

"We are limited as to what we are capable of projecting. Besides, that little hell world seems ripe for collapse; we can undoubtedly do more damage in person. Plus, Wu won't be expecting it."

"Why deceive him? You gave him a choice to go down with the ship or to save himself and expedite the inevitable. It's a no-brainer, right? I mean, you even let him stew in it. That was a stroke of genius, if you ask me."

Theory basked in Simeon's approval. "Tell me why."

"You left him a choice to stay or join us but let him think on it within the confines of a collapsing world. He thinks about it and as he realizes he can't beat you, he should take the offer. There is no doubt he will flip on that shithole to survive."

Theory's smile expanded to Cheshire Cat levels. "Smart boy. I bet you feel smarter in your new self."

"I do. I was concerned when I saw the state of the poor creature you brought back from the other world. I thought he would slow me down, but now I realize I am complete. I feel stronger than ever!"

Theory put a fatherly hand on Simeon's shoulder, "And once we collapse these two worlds and let my new one fill that space, my boy, the strength you feel now will pale in comparison."

Simeon hardly believed that could be possible. It was as if everything had slowed down. That slow motion pace allowed him the mental capacity to understand more, and process faster. Bu that wasn't all; physically he felt more alive than ever. It felt, as if there was nothing he couldn't do.

"You ready?" Theory asked.

Simeon nodded. Theory used his finger to trace a door in the air, and sure enough, one materialized as if it had always been there. The strange cosmic portal was just there—no walls supported it. The wood existed, as if it were imaginary, but it was real. Theory twisted the knob and pushed the portal open, and there were stairs leading down.

"After you," Theory instructed.

"Down? Why down?" Simeon asked.

"I think you know the answer to that."

Simeon looked at Theory. He didn't know, but he nodded regardless and took the first step down. It was a spiral staircase, and inside it was dark, but somehow his senses guided him without his feeling anxious or concerned that he couldn't see. Perhaps it didn't matter; now that he had been made whole, everything was going to be just fine.

He could hear something as he went further and further down into the darkness. There were clinks, sounds of the wind blowing dust, and an occasional faint scream. Even though Simeon knew he was descending to the hell that was the 5-Gen, the absence of sight and the presence of sound did make the trip down a bit more daunting.

Finally, as if he walked through a curtain at a theater, he stepped onto the stage of the grey, dead-looking world. It seemed even more desolate, actually feeling the unstable terrain underfoot. It looked worse than he had remembered, but he hadn't been on the outside, only in Wu's office. It appeared that they had patched rips in the fabric of their world. People were suspended in the amber-colored compound.

There was, surprisingly, no activity on the outside of the place. Just people suspended, and a bit of grey dust propelled by the wind. A strong preternatural gust came too, but when he turned to look, it was Theory; apparently when someone arrived via cosmic portal, the wind picked up.

"Not much of a welcoming committee," Theory said.

"You were expecting one?"

"Not really, but I *am* surprised there is no one about. It is curious."

"Look at this place—would you stand around out here? There are people suspended in whatever they came up with to patch the tears in their world."

Theory shrugged and then began walking. Simeon followed. The place reeked of desolation and desperation. The buildings seemed abandoned, although that may have been more of their nature—the two outerworld men knew Wu had a large population of prisoners, and undoubtedly these windowless, warehouse-type buildings was where they were housed. But what struck the two strangers as odd was the lack of guards patrolling outside the warehouses. It was mountainous terrain around the 5-Gen. In theory, guards were probably not necessary at all.

Then it happened: a rip in the world, about 200 feet away from Simeon and Theory. It sounded like an explosion when it happened, the shockwave pushing them back a bit.

"This isn't right," Theory said.

"What do you mean?"

"That isn't how it happens. My creation slowly pushes both worlds so that they rip, not explode—no, this is something else entirely. Someone is up to something."

They didn't move. They just stared at the shimmer of the hole in between worlds—that is, until Eli walked through. He was followed by one Selena, and then the other one, and she was followed by two armed Black syndicate assholes in tactical gear.

"Holy shit," Simeon said.

Theory remained silent but stared. Part of him pined for one of the Selenas, and the other part felt the opposite of whatever pining is. His lover and his enemy in the same package, finally sharing the same time and space. The irony wasn't lost on him. The one Theory had become murderous to find his love and failed; now to see her again under such auspices was unreal.

Selena White rushed up to Theory, and Eli came to Simeon.

"What did you do?" Selena asked him.

"What does that matter?"

Selena White touched the side of Theory's face that corresponded with the white-haired side. There was a hint of softening, but the black-haired side's hand knocked her hand away.

"So, you are gone..." Selena White said, bowing her head.

Eli was looking at Simeon. Perhaps it was a fear of the same rejection. Perhaps it was that Eli saw the difference in Simeon, despite the lack of a similar superficial marker as Theory. Either way, he didn't want to approach. Selena Black felt differently; she grabbed Selena White and led her away in an act of feminine solidarity.

"What do you want here?" Selena White asked, turning around.

Simeon and Theory watched them in silence. Perhaps it was their extrasensory perceptions warning them that these two parties, despite being in the same place at the same time, wanted altogether different things.

"You could be like us," Theory offered, finally.

"Why would we want that?" Selena Black asked.

"Why wouldn't you?" Simeon chimed in, looking directly at Eli.

Eli couldn't help but smile. He didn't know always what he wanted, but if there was one thing he was certain of, it was his feelings for Simeon.

"Yes, why wouldn't we?" Eli said to the two Selenas.

The two women looked at Eli incredulously. He returned the stare, tilting his head ever so slightly that one might have thought they imagined the movement.

"Then join us, and lose the armed assholes," Theory ordered.

Eli nodded, more at the Selenas but enough so that Theory and Simeon assumed he was just in agreement.

"What are you doing?" Selena Black mouthed.

"WHAT ARE YOU DOING?" Theory screamed.

"There is no way you could have heard me," Selena said.

"That is exactly why Eli is correct. We can make you like us. You can join the winning side. All is lost here, and there, but not everywhere. You can have heightened perceptions, all your senses will be turbocharged, you will never age, and you cannot die."

Theory approached the two Selenas. Simeon followed. He looked at Eli and nodded.

"What he says is true. It is like nothing I have ever experienced."

"I can see that," Eli said. "I am in—tell me how."

"You were always a good soldier, Eli. We have been waiting for you," Theory said to him. "We could be together again, if you are on board, Selena."

Both versions of Selena looked at him. They were afraid to say no, but also afraid to say yes.

"Why are you here, Elysium?" Selena White asked.

"Why are you here, Selena?"

Selena Black chuckled. "Really? This is what we are doing?"

"It was a rhetorical question," Theory said, looking at Selena Black.

The two groups stood there as if in some sort of standoff. Finally, Simeon spoke.

"You are here to try to work with this place and see if you can save your world. We are here to negotiate the end of it, and yours will follow. It's the same idea, just opposing philosophies—but we can save you and offer a better life, an infinite life, an unparalleled life."

"We are in," Eli spoke up.

Selena White nodded. "In."

Selena Black was the lone holdout, but eventually she capitulated too.

"Are you just buying time?" Theory asked.

"Would someone buying time do this?"

Selena turned with what seemed like supernatural speed and shot both the armed men right between the eyes. She turned back and looked directly at Theory. He nodded. She lowered and holstered her weapon.

"Can we get on with it?" Simeon asked Theory.

Theory was distracted by both Selenas. The idea of melding them and having a Hera to his Zeus became too much to bear.

"Change of plans—this new development changes the game," Theory said to Simeon.

"What about Wu?" Simeon asked.

"Wu isn't going anywhere, Simeon. We have new, exciting, more important work to do."

"What now?" both Selenas asked almost simultaneously.

"We are going home, to make everyone complete."

Theory used his finger to draw another door and then instructed Simeon to open it.

"Take your friend up; we will be right behind you."

"Come on, Eli; you will definitely want to see this." Simeon out-stretched his hand.

Eli felt warm inside. This was what he had hoped for. All he really wanted and needed was to be desired, and he felt that now, even if his mind kept telling him it wouldn't last. Eli took his hand and opened the mystical portal. The two disappeared inside it, leaving Theory and the two Selenas.

Theory was left alone with the two women, and although he couldn't wait for them to become one, he couldn't help but fantasize about the three of them together. He was still leery of Selena Black. Theory rationalized that she simply saw that there was no longer a point in fighting what was inevitable, or perhaps she just knew that Theory was the winning side. Then again, the idea of having his woman melded and next to him was beyond something even Theory could imagine. Theory and Selena would be the new Adam and Eve.

"This is what you both want?" Theory asked sheepishly.

The two women looked at each other, then at Theory, and both nodded. They seemed so in sync, it was hard to believe they hadn't already melded, and it was possible that in a cerebral sense they already had.

"Because there is no turning back—just so we are in full understanding."

Selena White walked past Theory and into the cosmic doorway. She touched his arm in a flirtatious manner as she did and said: "Why would we turn back? I belong to you: I always have, and so has she, in some way."

Theory smiled as Selena White stood in the doorway. They both looked to Selena Black. She was the last key to turn before going nuclear. She looked behind her into the abyss of the 5-Gen, as if to ask that world for some reason not to go with them, but when none came, she must have concluded that was her answer. And with that she took the same route as her counterpart, replete with the coquettish touch as she passed her benefactor. Theory followed, and when he reached the two women who stood in the doorway he offered them each an arm, and once they took it, the three moved as one into the pathway to Theory's creation.

CHAPTER 15

Wu paced nervously as his science team tried to surgically remove the blue men with the red tattoos from the compound they had created to hold their fading world together.

There was little he could do except hope that his men could figure out how to get these things out, and then if they could do that, they would be able to play their part in his plan—so much had to go right.

None of what they had in mind was proven or even tested; this was a Hail Mary with apocalyptic consequences. He stopped pacing for a moment and stared at the science team that were working at freeing the "custodians of the universes," as one man had dubbed them. He thought of his father, as he once stood in the same room when his father began to implement science as a part of what would become a staple of life in the 5-Gen.

His father had started the program, but Wu brought it home when he had become old enough and was given some responsibility. He was fascinated by the prospect of gaining more prisoners from wherever they could figure to travel. It had made his father proud; they soon discovered that their reach and power in the universe had grown. It was the equivalent of watering and growing plants with all the nutrients they could ever possibly need. The base became strong and the branches expanded.

The 5-Gen was kept in a nondescript, mountainous place. It was virtually inescapable from the inside out, and it wasn't so simple outside-in. Access to this slice of hell was possible only through extraordinary ways and means. Yet it could expand in space and influence, like the heart of a wicked being; this was the 5-Gen, and Wu had increased its position and strength in the cosmos.

Truth be told, they didn't know what they were, only that they were there to do it. How could the inhabitants, guards, or even its leaders know that they were the hub of cosmic pain and misery? That pain and misery fueled the 5-Gen.

But now that it was being torn apart, Wu was desperate not to be the Captain that sank the ship. Theory had given him an out, but he knew it was just a play to crush the 5-Gen faster. Still, as he paced, he realized he had little choice; he had to accept the offer, if for no other reason than to see what he was up against first hand, but also to see if he could buy time. Part of him wondered if these thoughts were just him being a coward— the ship was going to sink regardless, and maybe he just didn't want to go down with it.

Finally, he realized what he had to do. Pacing and watching his men work to reset the timeline wasn't helpful to anyone. In chess, sometimes you had to sacrifice pieces for the greater good. Wu was now prepared to do this.

Wu approached his head scientist. He realized that he didn't know his name. Wu thought at one point that he must have, but names weren't of much meaning to the Captain. You were either guard or prisoner to him. Perhaps that was part of the current problem.

"I seem to have forgotten your name," Wu said to the man in the white lab coat.

The scientist turned to Wu. He was surprised, not because Wu didn't know his name, but because he had asked him what it was. He tried to remember if Wu had ever used it, but realized it was conceivable he had never known it at all.

"James," the man told Wu.

"How are we looking here, James?"

"I have no timetable, sir, or any idea what these things will do once we free one or both of them."

"Understood, but I do want you to release them both, regardless of what you think the consequences may be," Wu told him.

James the scientist nodded, wearing a look of uncertainty.

"Good luck, James. We will need it." Wu turned and left the building.

The scientist didn't understand what had just happened, but he knew something was different. Still, he hadn't the time to let the thought gestate. He had to get back to work.

Outside in the 5-Gen yard, Wu took stock of its ever-changing landscape, people caught in the compound and even new tears in the fabric of his world. He wondered what might happen if he went through one of them, and part of this thought process was to fantasize being somewhere else. But he knew the truth about leaving and avoiding one's problems. He was aware that he would never be able to outrun them, only forget them for a little while. No, he had to do whatever he could to save this place, and perhaps all places. At least that was what he told himself as he walked through the desolation of the 5-Gen.

All the dormitories that held the prisoners had been locked down. There were five dorms altogether, and they were shut and locked from the outside. It was not exactly safe for them inside; should there be a fire or some other emergency, they had no means of escape. It had proven tragic in the past. One whole dorm ended up extra crispy from a fire started by accident. "The fires of hell burned hot," was what Wu said at the time. They built another dorm and replaced the dead miserable prisoners with new prisoners, and that was it. As if all that was important was the misery— it didn't matter who provided it.

The guards had been told to stay in their barracks as well. The only difference was that they weren't locked in. They would stay put, grateful for a free pass to be lazy, sleep, or play cards. They had more freedom than the inmates, but they were prisoners, too.

Wu went to the first dorm. If he hadn't known it was overstuffed with people, it would have seemed like a deserted warehouse. It was locked from the outside. He used a key to open the outer gate and raised it to enter. The smell was unmistakable: sweat and body odor slammed Wu in the face as he entered. He almost choked on the thickness of the air, but he went in anyway. He opened the barred gates, too. Inside it was dank, and as soon as the prisoners saw him, they scrambled to get to their bunks, cowering at the sight of the Captain.

Wu stood and was ashamed of himself for a moment, but that pity party ended soon. He was there for benevolent reasons, for a change.

"The doors to your dorm are open. I will be doing the same for the other dorms. You are free."

The Captain stood waiting for the inmates to rush out, but they did not move. They remained still.

"You can leave! It's OK. Go outside!" Wu pleaded.

The Captain left in frustration, but found the same when he repeated the process in the other dorms. He stood outside for a moment, facing the buildings that housed the recently freed prisoners. No one came out. This was the result if his tyranny—even when freed, his wards weren't free. Perhaps one never is truly unencumbered by the circumstances that their life has guided them into; we merely put on whatever front we can manage that tells us we actually have some control over our destiny.

The last stop he made was to the guards' quarters. They all stood up nervously as Wu materialized in the doorway. He never came to the officers' dorm. If they hadn't been so nervous he was there, they might have realized straightaway that something was amiss. They stood at attention, saluting Wu with such rigidity that they appeared to be statues.

"At ease, men," Wu told his men.

They stopped saluting but remained rigid.

"I have reopened the dorms. The prisoners are being allowed out, although they seem hesitant to do so. If you men choose to leave the barracks and see a prisoner brave enough to go out there, they are not to be beaten, or detained at all. Leave them be, is that understood?"

"SIR, YES, SIR," came the thunderous response.

"Good," Wu said before saluting.

The men returned the salute, and Wu turned and left. When he did, some of the men turned to each other wearing quizzical looks; others could not have cared less.

Wu went back out into the yard, which was still barren. A rip in the fabric of the world startled him as it opened too close for comfort, but he braved it and returned to his office.

Once inside, he took out the bottle of liquor he barely had looked at in years, for the second time in the same day. He didn't bother with a glass. He looked out from his perch into the yard and saw that it was still empty. Wu looked at the desolate, empty yard. It mirrored the way he felt inside.

The Captain took a heavy swig from the bottle. He closed his eyes as the burn crept down his throat. When he opened them, he saw that one of the prisoners had dared to test the uncertain waters of newfound freedom. He looked about like a curious animal insecure with his surroundings. Normally, Wu would have enjoyed the torture of the fear the inmates were feeling. The fear of the unknown was always the worst. And for the first time, Wu himself was in an unknown, and he was empathetic.

"Come on, you are free," Wu said, taking another swig.

He watched as another prisoner, seeing the success of the other, come out, and then another. Some guards also emerged. The dynamic had utterly changed. Wu wondered if it would end this way, or if he might succeed in rewriting history.

CHAPTER 16

Eli looked at his other. He was on the slab, just as Simeon had experienced. Simeon stood next to him, watching what his face must have looked like when he stood in the same spot.

"This is what you want for me, and us?" Eli asked.

Simeon looked behind him. Theory had not yet returned. Undoubtedly, he was dealing with the two Selenas. That was most certainly a mess—two personas rather than the one.

"I was skeptical too, Eli. I did it to buy time, but I feel more alive than ever. My senses are off the charts. Now, all I can say is that I am so glad I did it, and I think you would be too." Simeon paused. "I understand the trepidation, but the Theory from the other side is brilliant in ways his other was not. I think he is on to something here."

"What do I do? He looks—well, dead."

"Theory will care of all that and make you whole, just like he did with me."

"Where is he?"

"Oh, my friend, the poor asshole is dealing with not only the same woman, but two of them. I really empathize."

Eli laughed. "Yeah, me too."

Just then, a door appeared and it flung open. Out came the two Selenas and one Theory. Selena Black entered first; she drank in the surroundings.

Selena White was back to being under Theory's spell. They held hands.

"It's beautiful, Elysium," Selena White said.

"Have a look around."

Selena White moved to the window, amazed at the cosmos. Selena Black joined her, looking over her shoulder at Theory, who joined Eli and Simeon at the silver slab that held Eli's other.

"You ready for what is next?" Black asked White.

"Do we have a choice?"

They turned and looked out upon the stars, each undoubtedly wondering what was next and what would be left of them when next became now.

Behind them, Eli was uncertain about what he was about to do. Part of him was just so happy to be with Simeon, and he felt wanted. He realized that that is all most people want—just to know there is someone there, anyone, who will care about them and to whom they can return the care. Someone, anyone who was special, and that one was special too, a mutual feeling of being wanted. It was like a drug, and Eli was high enough to drink the Kool-Aid of this new world and its new ways.

"Ready?" Simeon asked

"It's safe, right?" Eli said, looking at his dead, gaunt other.

"It was same for me, and here I am, twice the man I used to be. I want that for you and us."

"What do I do?" Eli asked

"Lie down next to him. It will be easier like that," Theory chimed in.

Simeon touched Eli's face and nodded. Eli got on the slab with the corpse. As it turned out, that was the worst part of it. Theory touched both the living and the dead, and the two became one. Eli took a deep breath, as if he had been held underwater. He sat up suddenly. Eli looked at his arms, as if he couldn't believe they were attached. He looked back to see he was now alone on the sliver slab, but hopped off and moved around with greater dexterity than he had ever felt.

"Wow! Yes! Amazing!

The Selenas turned and saw that there was one Eli now. They observed how he looked fully realized, somehow, as if he were supercharged by an unseen ethereal light.

"Doesn't look so bad," Selena White said

"I never imagined any version of me that was so fucking optimistic. Let's get this over with."

Selena Black moved toward Simeon, Theory, and the new Eli. She turned to White, and said, "You coming?"

White nodded and followed. Theory wore a look of excitement. The idea of his complete self with hers was almost overwhelming for him.

"Lie on the table?" Black asked.

"Yes. You will feel different after the meld, better to acclimate slowly," Theory answered.

Black lay down, White followed suit, and Theory made the two Selenas one.

Eli threw his arms around Simeon and kissed him hard. Everything felt amazing, like some sort of wonder drug they were all on. It was pure bliss, in fact; if they could bottle it and sell it, that's what they would call it, Bliss. But Theory didn't have to bottle it—he could make it. He commended himself for being the master of a new universe that was so perfect. His population of this place was growing; he had advanced the human race beyond what was ever deemed possible.

Selena sat up slowly. The meld had yielded almost a copy of the former White, except she had two wisps of white in her otherwise raven hair. Selena adjusted quickly and hopped off the table with the dexterity of a trained gymnast.

She looked at her arms and legs as if taking her first steps, which in fact she somewhat was. Then she salaciously threw her arms around Theory's neck and kissed him passionately.

"Lot of that going around," Eli quipped.

Selena purred.

Then came a voice from a distance, but it was there—someone was calling for Theory. Of course, a normal person wouldn't be able to hear this otherworldly call, but these people were anything but normal.

"What is that?" Eli asked.

"Someone is calling your name, Elysium," Selena added.

"He has made up his mind," Simeon commented.

"I am only surprised it took this long—be good lads, and go collect his other."

"Who?" Selena asked.

"I am surprised you don't recognize the voice," Theory said.

"It can't be."

"I assure you, it is. I made him an offer he couldn't refuse. He gets to live in exchange for the surrender of his little hell. That space belongs to us."

Theory drew a door with his finger and instructed Eli and Simeon to find Wu's other.

"How do we get back?" Eli asked.

"Simeon knows what to do, don't you?"

"I think so," he said, using his finger to draw a door.

Theory smiled. "That for me?"

"Yes, it is," Simeon responded

"I am proud of you, Simeon. All of you are exceeding my expectations a hundredfold."

Theory took Selena by the hand and they disappeared through the door, and Eli and Simeon went through theirs.

The room had a strange loneliness with no one in it, but that didn't last long. Simeon and Eli returned first. with Wu's other. He was chubbier than his counterpart, but no less feisty. He bucked the two men as they held on to him until the door was gone.

"Where am I? What is this place?" Wu's counterpart demanded.

"It will all be clear soon enough," Simeon told him.

The other Wu looked at the cosmos. He was captivated. Selena and Theory came back too, with the 5-Gen Wu. He was in full dress uniform and looked bulkier then before.

Wu's other turned and saw the Captain. The two men came together, looking at each other as if they were looking through a mirror.

"It is going to be OK," the Captain said.

"What the fuck is going on?" his counterpart asked.

"Don't worry; it will be over soon," the Captain reassured him.

"Yes, it will be," Theory echoed.

"Just not the way you think!" Wu said

"What are you talking about?" Simeon asked.

"He is just prattling on about nothing. Fuck it, I was going to meld him—you know what? Fuck him. I don't need him. Just the space that his world takes."

Wu ripped off his jacket. He was wearing a bomb vest. The room got quiet, but that soon ended. Theory started laughing.

"You believe that will do something here?" Theory chuckled.

Wu looked around nervously. It happened later than he thought, but it did happen—the lightning zipping locally on two opposite ends of the room, and then they appeared: the Alpha and the Omega, the powder-blue, red- tattooed keepers of the cosmic peace. They took in the room, obviously confused as to what wrong they were supposed to right.

The Omega started first and moved preternaturally fast to Eli. Eli stared back at the creature, obviously overconfident in his newly melded self. The creature made short work of the boy, instinctively grabbing both his arms and tearing him in half.

"NOOOO!" Simeon said rushing at the Omega.

The creature tossed him aside as if he were an insect being flicked off by an overpowering finger, but the Omega had another problem; his counterpart, the Alpha seemed more intent on attacking him than he was on ripping the melded set into their deaths.

The Alpha tackled the Omega, and they twisted and turned. Simeon yelled at Theory.

"I thought we were immortal!"

"I am just as surprised as you are. I can fix it, but these fellas are a priority, as you might guess; they appear to have some intense power unique to them and dangerous for us."

The two blue creatures rolled to a wall, where they got upright. The Alpha had the Omega pinned, and Theory rushed at them using his newfound power to meld them. The two became one, and the fighting stopped. The combined creature fell over from being overstimulated by becoming one. He stood, finally looking at Theory until deciding he was an insect that needed flicking too. He sent Theory across the room, where he slid to Wu's feet.

Wu smiled at Theory and dove on top of him before detonating the vest. The new universe created by Theory went supernova, as if the most powerful nuclear weapon ever created had just been detonated. The nascent timeline was consumed by explosive light until it was no more.

EPILOGUE

Selena and Theory stood on top of the skyscraper. They each held a flute of champagne. It was a snapshot of a couple in love. They stood on the precipice of the building, as they looked out to the city night's beautiful illumination. They probably thought it was all for them, and perhaps in the moment, it was.

"It was a good idea to come up here, Selena. It's private, and I can't imagine a better view."

"I am glad you like it, Elysium."

"I would like it if you were a little less close to the edge."

Selena smiled and drank from her glass. "Stop worrying so much. Come over here."

Theory drank from his flute too, draining the champagne. He couldn't resist her, even if the idea of heights scared the crap out of him.

Selena lifted up the bottle, showing Theory he would be rewarded for doing what she asked. It did the trick, as he offered his empty glass that she filled.

"I am having déjà vu," he told her.

"I can't say I am surprised."

"You too?"

"Not exactly. Look out at the city, Elysium, and drink your champagne."

Theory smiled at Selena. "It couldn't be more beautiful, but it is so because you are here."

"That's sweet, Elysium," she said to him.

They both looked out over the edge, and then Selena pushed Theory off the building.